I0537094

THE U.G.I. IS HEAVEN!

"How did it all start?" she murmured. She was a blonde mopsy, all curves, all breasts and thighs, who made his eyes swim with visions of superheated sexual exercise. Yet all she seemed to want from him was an explanation of the Universal Guaranteed Income.

"Well, back in the twentieth century," he explained. "Bellman of the Rand Corporation predicted 2% of the work force would be able to produce all the country could consume by the year 2000 and . . ."

"And here we are," she said.

"Right, therefore, even if we laze around we're still entitled to the U.G.I."

"Wizard," she said. "The U.G.I. is heaven, but there's something even better."

"What?"

"Don't roach me, funker," she said. "And don't shirk off in your electro-steamer. This mopsy wants to poke."

She kissed him tenderly.

COMMUNE 2000 A.D.

MACK REYNOLDS

WILDSIDE PRESS

All rights reserved.
Copyright © 1974 by Mack Reynolds.
This book may not be reproduced in whole or in part, by
mimeograph or any other means, without permission.

Chapter One

When Theodore Swain awoke he didn't, customarily, open his eyes immediately. He was a vivid dreamer and invariably took a few moments to orient himself. He was, he decided, obviously in his own bed and in his own home. The day before he had spent largely at his studies, to the extent that he had eaten his evening meal in the community restaurant rather than take the time to prepare his own food, which was his wont. He was sleeping nude, which brought back to him the balance of the previous evening, after having finished dinner.

Nora, or was her name Norma?

He opened his eyes and looked at the pillow next to him.

Her short-cut hair was blond, most likely not naturally, and her eyes were very blue and at the moment were trained on him, an element of mocking there. Her nose was too small but she had perfect ears and a pouting, provocative mouth. The single sheet that covered them both hid her figure, but it came back to him now in a rush. She was a plump, much-curved girl, with possibly the most lush breasts he had ever enjoyed, the nipples so delicately pink that he had at first suspected cosmetics.

Ted said, "Good morning."

1

She ignored that, brought forth bare arms and stretched languidly. She looked at him, grinned a cat grin and said, accusingly, "Where did you learn that last position you talked me into? It was wizard, once you got onto the hang, but where'd you learn it?"

He said, "You'll never believe this, but actually it's depicted on the wall of a Mayan temple in Bonampak, in southern Mexico."

She said, remembering lasciviously, "It's the first time I ever did it standing up. Jim used to tell me I was going to get calluses on my ass from lying on my back so much."

Ted laughed. In actuality, he had always rather dreaded the morning after the lay before. What was the old wheeze? Before, you'd drink your coffee out of it, and afterwards you wouldn't spit in it. However, he had always forced himself to rise to the occasion.

He said, "That same Mayan position, by the way, is also depicted in stone carvings on the Hindu temple at Khajuraho and the Sun Temple at Konarak, so man in his infinite research into the subject evidently came up with the same results, half a world apart."

He thought about it, staring up at the ceiling, his hands behind his head. "I've always wondered where the so-called *normal* position ever got the name. The most-often utilized position of the Romans was with the woman sitting astride the man, the same as the Japanese do today. It gives the woman more control of the situation and a better chance at orgasm, particularly if the man is considerably larger or heavier than she is."

She yawned languidly. "I like it any way. Well, except for anal entry."

"Then you're lucky you didn't use to live in Peru back in Mochica-Chimu days. Sodomy and fellatio were so universal that it's a mystery how the culture ever propagated itself."

"You mean they were all queeries?"

"According to what you mean by 'queerie,' I suppose. They used to show their sex scenes on their pot-

2

tery. Hundreds, even thousands, of these came down to us, in spite of the fact that they were a culture that preceded the Incas. There are some, but few, of these pots that show a man and woman in ordinary intercourse. More often he is either sodomizing her, or she is practicing fellatio on him. The thing is, the women invariably are illustrated as enjoying what they are doing, and, in those days, the women were the tribal potters, so they were portraying themselves."

"When you said sodomy, I thought you meant boys."

"No, surprisingly enough, not a single pot comes down to us indicating that there was any homosexual connotation. The partners were invariably men and women."

She looked at him in deprecation. "Some professor you turned out to be. What a subject to be an authority on."

"I'm not a professor."

"Oh, I thought you were. Over at the university city."

He said, an edge of bitterness in his voice, "No. Actually, I'm a student. I've got my doctor's degree in ethnology and am working toward my academician's, if I can ever come up with a dissertation that's acceptable. Then, possibly, at the next job muster I'll be selected to teach—at long last."

"What's ethnology?" she said, obviously not really caring.

He recited, "Ethnology, the branch of anthropology which utilizes the data furnished by ethnography, the recording of living cultures, and archaeology, to analyze and compare the various cultures of mankind. In short, social anthropology which evolves broader generalizations based partly on the findings of the other social sciences."

"Wizard. A real jazzer. Now I know. What's anthropology?"

"The science of man and his works," he said briefly. "I specialize in pre-Columbian Mexican cultures, sub-

3

specialization, the Aztecs, sub-subspecialization, the Aztecs at the time of the Spanish conquest."

She squirmed, allowing the sheet to drop to the point where one well-rounded breast peeked out. "Well, why do you bother? From what you say, they turned you down on your first job-muster time. They must have, if you're your age. You must be over thirty. Your chances of being picked up for a job at a later muster are on the slim side, aren't they?"

"Yes," he said, his voice low. He thought about it and when he spoke again his voice was lemonish. "I suppose it's the educational system we have now. From practically kindergarten they begin seeking out your interests and abilities, testing, testing, testing. With me, it came out early, a special tendency toward history and the other social sciences. By the time I was in high school, I began concentrating on archaeology and anthropology. It became the dominating interest in my life. And the further I went, the more of a driving force it was. So, why did I continue to study, even after taking my doctorate, and failing to be selected in the yearly job muster? I wanted to teach, or work in field expeditions. I wanted to utilize all that I had developed to such an extent. I ate, breathed and slept anthropology."

"But they turned you down," she said reasonably, letting the sheet slip down to the point where both of her greatest claims to transcendent beauty were exposed. "So what spins?"

He shrugged in irritation. "The academician degree is all but a guarantee of a teaching job. They're so difficult to take now, the requirements are so stiff that you're almost automatically selected for teaching by the data-banks computers, if you have one."

"What's holding it up?" she said, displeased because he was ignoring her obviously available charms.

"I haven't been able to find an acceptable subject for a dissertation. I'm still a candidate, but my director keeps turning down every subject of research I dream up." He looked over at her. "What do you do, Nora?"

4

She said, "I don't do anything. When I got out of school and the computers came up with my Ability Quotient, I was evidently best suited to be a secretary. So were about five million other girls who were placed on the job-muster list. I must have wound up pretty near the bottom. And they only selected about fifty thousand that year. It's a job category rapidly going out, what with these new autosecretaries. So I just collect my Universal Guaranteed Income and work at having a good time."

"I see. Along with nine-tenths of the rest of the country."

"So they say."

In actuality, the subject irritated him, though he couldn't exactly put his finger on the reason. He switched the line of conversation. "What happened to you and Jim? I thought you were tied up together rather firmly."

Pretending to be bothered by the heat, she pushed the bedsheet completely from her, revealing belly, hips, the pubic area and her very good legs. Ted Swain had been right. She wasn't a true blond.

She said, offhandedly, "Oh, Jim is the great-sports-man type. Hunting, fishing and all. He was always hauling me along. I'm more a guzzle, bed, fun-and-games type. So finally I told him to shirk off." She looked at him from the side of her eyes. "Talking about fun and games, do you know any more of those fancy Indian positions?"

He laughed and swung his long, scrawny legs out of the bed and to the floor. "Ever so many, but you'll have to take a rain check. I've been in bed too late as it is. You can have the bathroom first. I'll start getting some breakfast organized."

She pouted slightly but accepted the rejection. There would undoubtedly be other occasions to enjoy the far-out innovations of the accomplished professor, or whatever he was.

She said, "You mean you cook your own breakfast?

5

What's the matter with the automated kitchens, or the autochef over at the restaurant?"

"Too automated," he said, reaching for his robe.

She got up too. On her bare feet, he realized how truly small she was. In bed, she had seemed taller, and the day before, when he had picked her up, she had been wearing rather high-heeled Cretan Revival slippers.

She said, "The thing about an autochef is, you get perfect food every time."

"That's the thing, all right," he told her, defending his hobby as an amateur chef. "Exactly the same thing, every time. Perfection, in every recipe on the tapes. For me, I like a little variety. I like my scrambled eggs slightly softer or slightly harder, from day to day. I even don't mind them burned, occasionally, just to prove that all isn't automated and perfect in present-day society. Now shirk off to the bathroom."

She laughed and hurried in that direction, her pink bottom jiggling so girlishly that he momentarily considered reversing his decision to start early at his studies. But no. When you are your own disciplinarian, with nobody else to see that you keep your nose to the old grindstone, you can't afford to make exceptions. After a time, they cease being exceptions.

Ted headed for his kitchen. He was going to whomp her up a breakfast she'd never forget. How about eggs in Malaga wine and black butter? It was his own recipe.

In actuality, Nora wasn't his usual cup of tea. She was completely amoral and, in her time, had probably been in bed with every man in the community. Ted, who was possibly ten years her senior, had been born in an averagely traditional family, and some of the old mores had worn off on him during childhood. The new permissiveness had already begun and by the time he had reached maturity he'd accepted the rapidly changing standards, but in his background there was still that which made him a wee bit straitlaced as compared to

6

Nora's generation, which had never known the old concepts.

By the time they finished breakfast, he had grown weary of her vapid chatter and made no protest, nor no future date, when she prepared to leave. He was slightly chagrined at the fact that she hadn't commended him upon the Eggs Malaga—they had turned out perfectly.

She wore Bermuda shorts and the Cretan Revival slippers but had evidently decided that it was sunny enough, even at this early hour, to go topless back to her own place, and had thrown her blouse in the disposal chute in the bath. She went up on her tiptoes, kissed him briefly, said, "It was fun, Tom." She added mischievously, "Don't forget the raincheck. Maybe you'll convert me into becoming a student of the Indians."

The door opened for her when she approached.

He said, as she bustled through it, "The name's Ted."

She looked at him over her shoulder and grinned. "And I'm Marsha, not Nora."

He grunted at that and went on back into the bedroom and through it to the bath for his shower. Shaving wasn't necessary since he'd had his facial hair removed several years past. He had always hated to shave, even with a depilatory. Some of his friends had given him the argument that if beards ever came back in, he'd be sunk, but Ted Swain was no follower of the fads and he wouldn't have grown a beard no matter what the style.

His was a craggy face, certainly less than handsome in the accepted taste, both his ears and mouth being much too large. And there was an intense something about his eyes that had an inclination to throw off his acquaintances and colleagues. It took time to become friends with Ted Swain; he didn't have many. Those he did have were close. He had qualities down beneath.

Marsha had been right about going topless, he decided. It was going to be a warmish day even though autumn was already upon them. He selected a kilt from his closet and wrapped it around his waist. He didn't bother to don footwear.

He went on back into his living room and through it into the small study. It was small, since there was no reason for it to be otherwise. Save for a few reference books, the room was devoid of the atmosphere formerly considered required by a scholar. The furniture consisted solely of one bookshelf, and one chair behind a desk, the top of which was an autoteacher; its screen connected with the National Data Banks. There was an additional library-booster screen to one side, so that he could consult more than one source at a time, a TV phone, and a voco-typer. The reason he had any reference books at all was that he found it quicker, sometimes, to manually look up, say, a word in a dictionary, rather than dialing a book from the data banks.

He went over to a shelf and brought down his bottle of stimmy and took one of the pills. It wasn't Ted Swain's field, and he had no real idea of the make-up of the ganglioside, other than that it contained magnesium pemoline. That it worked, he did know. He would be mentally stimulated for at least two hours; his I.Q. more than doubled, his ability to retain tripled. What was it someone had said? I.Q. isn't enough. You have to have push as well. A lazy genius isn't one. Well, stimmy gave you the push.

He went back to the desk, sat down before his screen and activated it. He looked at it and sighed. Stimmy pill or not, he was already past his peak of mental aptitude. The human brain begins to lose its ability to absorb at approximately the age of twenty-five. The new kids coming up in the field of ethnology had more on the ball than he did. He had more experience, more accumulated knowledge, than they, but their Ability Quotients were higher.

On the subject dial he dialed Ethnology, Mexico, the Aztecs, and then from the Peabody Museum Reports of Adolph F. Bandelier, and to the second report, *On*

8

the Social Organization and Mode of Government of the Ancient Mexicans. It had been written in 1878 and for his money was still the definitive work on the Aztec Confederation, a sleeper forgotten by many modern ethnologists.

Usually Ted Swain studied in Interlingua, every work in the National Data Banks, Library Division, having been translated into the international language, but this time he stuck to the originals since he sometimes distrusted *any* translation. The computer translaters, in particular, sometimes missed up on such matters as idiom.

He flicked the pages until he arrived at the point where he had left off the day before, a quotation from Fray Toribio de Motolinia's *Historia de los Indios de Nueva Espana.* Motolinia had come a bit late on the scene but he had done a fantastic amount of research into the nature of Montezuma's Government.

His desk TV phone buzzed and he looked up in irritation. Damn it doubly, he wished that he had a proper escape room in which to study. He had the phone on a number-two priority, ruling out all but important calls, or governmental announcements, but that wasn't enough to guarantee his absolute privacy.

He flicked off his autoteacher and activated the phone.

To his surprise, it was Academician Franz Englebrecht, head of the department of ethnology at the university city in which Ted Swain was enrolled, and his director of dissertation.

Ted hadn't even talked with him for almost six months when Englebrecht had turned down his suggestion of a dissertation based on the true population of Tenochtitlan, the old Aztec Mexico City.

Englebrecht beamed at him; the insipid smile irritated Ted Swain more than anything else about the man. Pompous, yes, an asshole, yes, but did the son-of-a-bitch have to *beam* at you in that condescending manner?

Ted said, "Good morning, sir."

9

"Good morning, Swain. Well, I'll not mince about. I think we have the theme for your dissertation, my boy. Can you come to my apartments immediately?"

"Why, yes sir, of course. But . . . but what is it?"

The other beamed again at him. "Not over the phone, Swain. We must run no chance of it leaking out. Some other candidate might see what a natural it is and publish before you could. We'll talk it over in the seclusion of my escape santuary."

Chapter Two

When the other's face had faded, Ted Swain leaned back for a moment in his chair and let first surprise and then emotion wash over him. At long last.

He shook his head, took a deep breath and came to his feet. He went on into the bedroom, and to his closet, and selected a white Yucatan type shirt-jacket. He looked down at his kilts and considered donning more conservative trousers. But no, the hell with it, he decided. Badly as he wanted to get along with his director of dissertation, he didn't want to toady to the man.

He brought forth a pair of high woolen socks, in the Scottish tradition, donned them and then a pair of comfortable loafers.

He brought out his pocket transceiver, touched the stud that activated the cover, and dialed for a single seater. He walked to the door and through it, when it automatically opened for him, and down the walk to the street.

His electrosteamer rounded a corner and smoothed up to the curb before him. It was an open car, as he had dialed, and instead of bothering to open the door he flung a long leg over the side and made himself comfortable behind the manual controls.

The controls were simplicity itself—an accelerator, a brake, the wheel. He put his pocket transceiver on the payment screen, so that the trip could be deducted from his credit account, touched the accelerator with his right toe and was off, heading for the entry to the underground expressway at the community center.

Ordinarily he preferred to drive on the surface, manually, but this time he was in a hurry to get to his destination. Before Englebrecht changed his mind, he thought wryly. But, besides that, he wanted to think without the distraction of driving.

At the community center, he waved a couple of times to friends in the tennis courts and the swimming pool, then drove up to the expressway autodispatcher, parked on the dispatch coordinator and flicked off the manual controls. He dialed his destination: the administration building of University City V11. The auto controls took over and the car smoothed forward. He knew from long experience that the ride would be twenty-two minutes, or, had he remained on the surface, at least an hour, probably more, according to traffic. The amount of traffic made no difference below ground.

His electrosteamer blended into the flow of cars, trucks, and buses on the slowest lane, faded over to the left into intermediate, and then into the high-speed lane. Ted closed his eyes and leaned back.

He hadn't the vaguest idea what his director of dissertation had in mind. And, frankly, he mistrusted him. He thought the man an incompetent. Supposedly, under present society, it was impossible for an incompetent to maintain his position. Supposedly, the computers of the National Data Banks checked out your Ability Quotient to the finest hair and unless you had the most ability to hold down the position in question you were bounced out by that man or woman who did possess the ability.

Ability Quotient. It had its beginnings, perhaps, in the early I.Q. tests such as had been given to school children and later military personnel, in the categories of general aptitude, mechanical aptitude and mathematical aptitude. But Ability Quotient went far beyond I.Q. The I.Q. tests had not and couldn't measure all-round intelligence, since there wasn't any such thing. But they were the beginning. Present-day society still utilized an upgraded form of the I.Q. tests, but they also tested for verbal ability, verbal fluency, numerical ability, spatial ability, perceptual ability, memory, speed of reflexes, accident proneness, digital dexterity, analogizing power, mechanical aptitude, clerical aptitude, emotional maturity, veracity, tone discrimination, taste sensitivity, natural charm, color blindness, accuracy, persistence, drive, neurosis, powers of observation, health, and a few other things.

All of the people of United America were given the tests, almost continually from the cradle to the grave, although in actuality they fell off after you had reached retirement age. In fact, if you wished, you need not take them any longer after that period was achieved. Many didn't. It gave them an inferiority complex to realize to what extent the young people coming up were doubling or even tripling their own, once proud, perhaps, Ability Quotients. It was a rapidly changing world.

Theoretically, on job-muster day, each year, the computers selected, from the data banks, the most suitable person for each job in the nation, on the basis of Ability Quotient, but there was more to it than that. Besides basic ability, experience was considered. And a man who had done superlative work on his job the preceeding year had a good chance of retaining it, even though another, fresh out of school, had a higher A.Q. But this was not always so. Selection was made frequently according to the position and level one achieved in the job hierarchy, and tenure counted more, particularly if one took booster courses in his field to keep him up on the latest developments.

His car swerved back into the intermediate speed lane, then over to the slowest, to emerge shortly onto a side road. About half a kilometer and it took a still narrower way and in a few moments entered the motor pool area of the administration building of the university city. It pulled up before the elevator banks and Ted Swain touched the door button so that he could get out. He said into the car's screen, "Dismissed," and it slid away to park itself until the computers summoned it for some other passenger.

Ted made his way over to the elevators that served the apartments on the high levels of the 110-story aluminum-sheathed twin-towered hi-rise building. Englebrecht lived in tower two, as did a good many other ranking professors and department heads. Not all of the school's faculty chose to remain in residence, in the somewhat sterile atmosphere of the ultramodern building, but a majority did. There was a certain element of status symbol involved.

Ted looked at the compartment's screen and said, "Theodore Swain to see Academician Englebrecht, apartment 355, tower two."

"Your identification, please," the screen said in its mechanical voice.

Ted had already drawn his pocket transceiver from his shirt jacket. He flicked open the cover and held it up against the screen, revealing his identity number, S-204-121645M.

"You are expected," the voice said and the elevator began to rise, accelerating at a constant rate, but not too quickly for comfort.

It slowly decelerated, stopped, then shunted off to one side, at a much slower pace.

It stopped again and the door opened and the screen said, "Apartment 355."

Ted stepped out and into the entranceway of Academician Englebrecht's quarters. He hadn't been there for some time and, once again the sheer luxury of the place impressed him greatly.

He stood there for a moment, waiting, and shortly a young man entered, very briskly. He was immaculately, though quite conservatively, dressed in brown tailored shorts, a checked, collarless shirt, reinforced with a Byronic cravat, and a lapelless jacket without pockets. His shoes were brown and very earnest; probably British import, Ted decided. He was a pale-faced, energetic type, with a certain supercilious quality. He wore a soft Van Dyke, his lips were too red, and Ted Swain suspected that he was a queerie. He was supposedly one of Englebrecht's secretaries and lived in the academician's quarters, which gave additional rise to Ted's snide opinions of his director of dissertation. Englebrecht was a life-long bachelor.

The secretary's name was Brian Fitz, and he said, "Ah, Doctor Swain, isn't it?"

There it was, the supercilious touch. Fitz knew damn well it was Swain, the elevator had automatically notified him of Ted's coming. Besides, they had met before.

"That's right, Fitz," Ted said. "The academician called about an hour ago saying he wanted to see me."

Fitz fluttered a hand in a gesture to be followed, and turned to lead the way, saying over his shoulder, "Certainly. He is in his escape sanctum."

Ted followed the other down a deeply carpeted hall. On the walls were several paintings which he suspected should have been in the university city's museum. Well, Englebrecht wasn't the only member of the upper reaches of the faculty to pull that one. The excuse was always that there wasn't room to hang them in the museum and otherwise they would be collecting dust in the basements. Once, as a younger man, Ted Swain had participated in a dig in Mexico and had returned proudly with several excellent specimens of Chipicuaro pottery, a ceramic mask and two figurines. He had, of course, presented them to the school museum, and was somewhat disillusioned later to spot the pre-Columbian artifacts displayed in the home of the head of the archaeology department.

They stopped before a massive wooden door and Brian Fitz murmured softly, "Doctor Swain, sir."

The door screen said, "Do come in," and the door opened.

Ted Swain was impressed, once more, with the room's magnificence.

Franz Englebrecht was sitting behind a desk which was impressively littered with papers, and devoid of TV phone, library booster, or any other electronic device of the present.

Very impressive, Ted thought lemonishly.

The other didn't bother to come to his feet to shake hands. He beamed and said, "Excellent, Swain. I must say, you are prompt."

"Good morning, sir," Ted said. You're goddamned right I'm prompt, he thought. You'd be prompt too, if you'd been waiting for this the better part of a decade. His eyes went about the room again.

It was an escape room fitted out by someone who didn't know how to pinch pennies and who wasn't expected to know how. It was large and square and the ceiling was high, high above. There was soft-piled rose broadloom on the baseboards, white metal venetian blinds and gold damask draperies at the windows and redwood paneling on the only wall that wasn't lined with shelves of books in rich bindings behind glass. A circular redwood stand in one corner supported a huge globe. Between two windows was the oversized desk at which the academician sat. It supported a dull bronze lamp.

Englebrecht saw the expression on his visitor's face and chuckled. "Rank has its privileges, my boy, even in a collectivist society. You see, to get the most out of us, ah, upper executives, we have to have facilities not required by those we direct."

"Would you call this a collectivist society?" Ted asked.

"Why, of course, I suppose so. I can't think of any more appropriate term. Some would call it socialistic, but practically every country remaining in the world calls itself socialistic, and hardly two of them but differ. The term is too elastic. It ranges from the Soviet Complex to North Africa, which is still primarily an aggrarian, Moslem society."

16

The older man looked at his secretary. "I suppose that it is too early for a drink," he said. "Brian, could you rustle up some coffee for Doctor Swain and myself?"

"Oh, yes sir." He turned briskly and was off to dial the beverage in the pseudokitchen.

"Have a chair, Swain, my boy," the director said. He beamed his jovial smile again, to his visitor's distress.

Ted Swain sat down in a leather chair across from his host's desk. "Needless to say, Academician Englebrecht, I was pleased to get your call."

"Of course, of course. I've had an eye on you for a long time, my boy. I've been racking my mind for years in your behalf."

Ted Swain tried to keep scepticism from his face and hoped that he was successful. Dissimulation wasn't his strongest point.

"Very kind of you, sir."

"The inspiration came just last night. To be perfectly honest, I checked it out with the data banks to see if any of my other candidates might be more highly qualified for the research." He smirked fondly at Ted Swain. "None of them came within an inch of touching your qualifications."

"Well, thank you, sir. But, well ... just what is this thesis?"

Englebrecht puffed his cheeks out slightly, as though he were about to astound his caller. "You are a particular student of Henry Lewis Morgan and Bandelier."

"Why, yes, I am."

"Very well, of course, of course. The two of them, in the 19th Century, specialized in the primitive clans which were the basis of society in Neolithic times."

"Gens," Ted muttered. "They called them gens."

"Of course, of course," the other said, patting a well-larded knee with a larded hand. "Communal society, eh? The family, the clan, the tribe."

It wasn't exactly the way Ted Swain would have put it.

Englebrecht said, "You are acquainted with the present communes which are springing up throughout the nation like mushrooms after a rainfall?"

Ted looked at him blankly. "Well, I've heard about them. I haven't had the opportunity to see or investigate the phenomenon."

Englebrecht beamed. "You will, my boy. Your theme will be a comparison of the present-day communes with the primitive communes of ancient society."

Chapter Three

Ted Swain stared at him. "What possible connection could there be?"

Englebrecht was impatient. "See here, my boy, if you aren't interested in this research . . ."

Ted said hurriedly, "Oh, it's not that. The . . . the concept is simply so new to me."

"Of course. However, you must admit that according to Morgan and Bandelier primitive society was communal. Based on the family, based on what amounted to an early form of communism. No such thing as private property. Often, even women were held in common."

The man obviously had no idea of what he was talking about. Ted said desperately, "But the present-day communes are not composed of related families, necessarily, and though perhaps some of them practice community ownership, that isn't necessarily the rule. It's . . . well, it's practically impossible to compare these modern developments in communal living with what pertained in Neolithic times."

Englebrecht smirked. "Are you so sure?"

Ted Swain stared at him again.

Englebrecht said, "I understand that you, yourself, live in what amounts to a commune."

Was the man completely drivel happy?

"Admittedly," the academician said, with a brush of a fat hand, "it is not a clan society. What *is* the basic idea of the town into which you have retreated?"

Ted said unhappily, "Possibly 'retreated' is valid, but I never thought of it as a commune. We're a community of possibly a thousand singles."

"Singles?" the other said triumphantly, as though he had gained a telling point.

"Why, yes. None of us are married, though some live together. We have approximately eight hundred homes with a community center. Most of us are people like myself, students, some working in the arts, bachelor types, both male and female, who have jobs but want privacy in their off hours. That sort of thing. But I wouldn't call it a commune."

He felt somewhat desperate. This was falling apart by the minute. The man was flat, he hadn't the vaguest idea of how things spun. How in the hell could he be holding down a department in a major university city?

"All right, very well, of course. Your commune, escaping from the pseudocities, stresses singles. Others stress doubles ..." Englebrecht chuckled lewdly "... of any sex. Some with children, some without. Others are so-called extended families, where every man is married to every woman and the children are the children of all. And, I submit, isn't that the communal society of most-primitive man?"

He didn't know what he was talking about, and here he was head of the goddamned department, Ted Swain told himself all over again.

Ted said, with care, "Well, something like that. However, although it's not my subject, I don't think very many of these present-day communes are based on the extended family. They're usually based on a community of interest."

"How do you mean?"

"Well, for instance, a new mobile town commune is shaping up in a camping area near where I live. I haven't been over but I've heard about it. There are already some two hundred trailers and other mobile homes. Their, ah, theme is the arts. It's a mobile art colony. You either have to be an artist, or be deeply interested in the arts. Other mobile towns, so I understand, might consist of none but elderly people, still others, sports-oriented people who take their town from one sporting event to the next."

Ted Swain thought about it for a moment, then continued, "Then up in the area they used to call Vermont, I know of an agricultural commune. Modern farming isn't practical in that area, as we know, so they had no difficulty getting permission from the Production Congress to take over several thousand acres. They farm it in the old manner, even using horses and mules rather than mechanical equipment. I suppose you might say they're glorified gardeners, rather than farmers, but that's their hobby, and that's the theme of their establishment."

Brian Fitz came in with the steaming cups of coffee, served first the academician and then his guest.

Englebrecht was saying, "Of course, fine. Very well. That is exactly what we want. Your task will be to seek out these various communes and find out all there is to find out about them. Acquire your material and then collate it. You might do several papers as you go along. Eventually, you will be able to put it all together and then write your dissertation, say some two hundred pages, comparing the ancient communes with those of the present. My boy, I absolutely guarantee you'll get your degree."

A tiny red light made itself evident on the academician's desk and he frowned.

"Confound it, is a man not even safe from interruption in his own escape sanctum? See who that is, Brian."

The secretary bustled out.

Ted Swain was frowning faintly at the patterns of sunlight on the floor. Finally he said, "Just what sort of material did you have in mind?"

His host rubbed plump hands together in satisfac-

21

tion. "Everything, my boy. Find out everything; what motivates them, what their goals are. Dig into their economics. . . ."

"Economics? What economics? They're practically all on Universal Guaranteed Income, just like the rest of us. One of the reasons they formed into these communes is that they weren't given jobs on muster day and banded together, retreating into their own hobbies or pleasures."

Brian Fitz reentered the room, followed by another man. He said, "Academician Dollar is calling, sir."

Franz Englebrecht came to his feet, beaming, his hand outstretched. "Ah, George. A pleasure to see you."

Ted Swain stood too. He had never met the man before but had seen him on TV broadcasts on occasion. George O. Dollar was this region's head of the National Data Banks, a position of no small importance. With the redivision of the former fifty states into more reasonable, easier-to-administer regions, a director of a regional section of the National Data Banks was an impressive rank.

The newcomer was cut from the same mold as was Englebrecht. That is, he was pushing sixty, was overweight in an era when few persons allowed themselves to be, was conservatively dressed and customarily wore an expression that in an earlier day would have been called that of a politician.

Dollar reached over the desk and shook Franz Englebrecht's hand. "We must get together more often. I was in the neighborhood and couldn't resist dropping by." He looked questioningly at Ted Swain. "I hope I'm not intruding."

"Not at all, not at all, George. Meet Doctor Theodore Swain, one of the candidates under my wing for the academician degree."

George Dollar shook Swain's hand and he and Ted mumbled through the usual amenities while Fitz brought up a chair for the newcomer.

Dollar laughed pleasantly. "An academician, eh? Well, I'll tell you, with the new teaching methods so many degrees are being taken that I wouldn't be surprised if, in the near future, the Education Guild will come up with a higher one, still more difficult to achieve." He laughed again, in deprecation. "Then we'd have Bachelor's degree, Master's, Doctor's, Academician's ..." He looked over at his friend. "What could we call the next one, Franz?"

"Zoroaster forbid," Englebrecht said jovially, reseating himself. "It was all I could do to make academician. It wasn't as easy as it is today, when we were struggling along, was it, George?"

Ted Swain said, "It's not as easy as all that today, either."

The data-banks head looked at him. "What's the subject of your dissertation, Doctor Swain?"

Ted Swain said unhappily, "Contrasts between primitive and modern communes."

"Fascinating. I'm anxious to see it when you publish."

"Very kind of you," Ted muttered.

"No, I mean it. It will be invaluable to me. I'm anxious to get such a work into the data banks."

Ted looked at him. "You mean it's a good idea?"

"Certainly it is from my viewpoint. Our coverage of the commune phenomenon is a farce. Any additional data we can get will be most welcome. And perhaps it will lead to others delving into them. Just what aspects of the commune culture were you going to investigate?"

Ted shifted slightly in his chair. "That was just what we were discussing when you entered, sir."

Englebrecht looked at the newcomer. "Any suggestions, George?"

The other grimaced thoughtfully. "Why, yes. And if Doctor Swain will contact me later, I'll have additional ones. I'll put some of my boys on it." He turned to Ted, who was now feeling considerably better about the whole thing. "The communes differ radically, you undoubtedly know. It is difficult to find any two that are

23

basically the same. Each has a different theme...."
There was that word again. "Each, uh, goes to hell in
its own way. And almost all of them cooperate very
poorly with the National Data Banks, and statistics in
general. Most seem in sullen revolt against the data
banks."

He made a gesture with both hands, as though in
despair. "Our civilization is based on data banks and
the computers. How can we serve these people if they
don't keep us informed?"

He pursed his lips in thought and cocked his head
slightly. "Almost any data on the make-up of these
communes is of value to us; their *raison d'être*, their
goals, their composition, so far as age groups, sexes,
political beliefs and ..."

"Political beliefs?" Ted said.

"Yes, certainly. An increasing number of the communards don't participate in even the civil elections.
Most aren't eligible to participate in the guild elections,
because they hold no jobs, but they don't bother to
vote in the civil elections, either. To put it bluntly,
they're anarchists."

Ted Swain looked at the data-banks man. "Under
our system, no person is obligated to vote. Nor, for that
matter, to submit statistics on himself to his data-bank
dossier."

"That is true, though I'm not sure that there shouldn't
be such requirements. For the individual's own good,
understand? For instance, your medical record.
Theoretically, from the time of your birth—even before,
since we have the records of your parents and often
your grandparents—every report on your health, every
time you consult a doctor, is filed away. Suppose you
are a resident of this Eastern area of our country but
take a trip out to the West Coast and have an accident.
Within moments, the doctor who treats you can have
your complete medical record."

"Admittedly," Ted nodded. "But on the other hand,
any National Security officer who busts you also has a
complete record of your criminal career."

24

Englebrecht laughed in deprecation. "Why not? Who in the world has a criminal record these days?"

"Some of those who live in the more far-out communes," Dollar replied wryly. "Crime might be at a minimum, nowadays, since we've dispensed with money, but there is still some, usually psychopathic. The data banks should have records, even of criminals, for the sake of the criminal. How can he be treated if we don't know what's wrong with him?"

Dollar was pursing his lips. He said, "It occurs to me, Doctor Swain, that you are in an ideal position to make your investigation. You'll be far more efficient than representatives from the data banks. They won't suspect you. You can pretend that you wish to join them. You're in the most favorable age group, have no present job position, are single—in short, an ideal recruit for any of a hundred or more of these communes."

Englebrecht beamed. "Of course, of course," he said. "Exactly what I had in mind."

They discussed it further, both of the older men making suggestions on just what Ted should seek out in his research. Both demanded that he keep in touch with them, and allow them to peruse his early papers. Both thought that they would have additional suggestions when they had mulled it over a bit.

When Ted left, the other visitor stayed on, obviously to chat about old times. Two sixty-year-old cronies, reliving their youths.

In the elevator, returning to the motor pool in the basements of the administration building, Ted worried it over. He had the damnedest feeling that, in spite of the manner in which the conversation had gone, Dollar had already known about his proposed dissertation before he had entered. That his dropping in and inadvertently meeting Ted was a put-up matter, rehearsed beforehand.

For one thing, how had George Dollar known that Ted Swain was both without employment and single?

No one had mentioned those facts, though Englebrecht knew of them.

The thing was that it didn't make sense. What possible reason could the two have to snowball him into researching the communes?

Chapter Four

When he arrived back at his home in the community of West Hurley, it was to receive a slap in the face.

Ted Swain was a bachelor. He had never been married. As it is sometimes with bachelors, he kept his establishment spotless. Everything had its place, everything was immaculate. It was a source of amazement to his feminine visitors, who usually expected unmade beds, dirty glasses and dishes, unswept floors and the rest. But not Ted Swain's.

Thus it was that when he entered he knew almost immediately that the place had been ransacked. The job had been neatly done, and obviously whoever had gone through the house had made an effort to disguise the fact. But it couldn't be hidden from Ted Swain. A writing stylo, which he invariably kept on the right side of his desk, was on the left. A file of his notes was not in exactly the same order as he had left it. There were other discrepancies.

Nothing seemed to be missing, nothing at all. But what could have been missing? He had nothing worth stealing. Petty crime and burglary were all but unknown in this age. Why steal when your Universal Guaranteed Income provided you with all you needed?

Mystified, he dialed the National Data Banks and requested a report on who had been recorded on his door identity screen that day. The computers automatically filed such information. It came in handy if you wanted to check on visitors who might have called while you were away from home.

He could only stare when the NDB reported that his identity screen had not recorded anyone.

He wandered around the house, his face twisted in disbelief. The intruder couldn't possibly have come in through the windows; they automatically locked when he left the house, unless he set them otherwise. Their glass was unbreakable, or nearly so, so it made no difference. And they weren't broken. The only entry was through the front door, or through the back, which led onto his Japanese-style rock garden. The back door, too, had been locked, and it also had an identity screen.

It was simply impossible. He *knew* the house had been searched, but by whom, and to what end, simply was unanswerable. He was a university scholar; he had no secrets, nothing of value beyond a few family keepsakes, meaningless to anyone else.

He gave up.

The stimmy he had taken that morning for studying had worn off, but he didn't take another. It was pushing lunch time.

However, he couldn't resist a quick initial approach to his subject. The enthusiasm of both of the older men had resolved some of his original misgivings. If the local head of the data banks thought a dissertation on the communes was a natural, who was Ted Swain to say him nay? He sat down at his library-booster screen.

He had difficulty locating the subject. Well, that wasn't quite the way to put it. In actuality, there was so precious little to locate that he couldn't believe it.

The National Data Banks supposedly contained all information available. The whole thing had begun back in the late 1960s when New Haven consolidated the city's files on individuals into a single data pool open to all town agencies. And Santa Clara County, in California, put all county residents into a computer bank, listing age, address, birth record, driver's license, voting and jury status, property holdings, occupation, health, welfare and police records.

The Federal Government hadn't been far behind them. In 1968 the Internal Revenue Service began the utilization of computers to collect income tax and there was a good deal more information on income-tax forms than pertained to income alone. Adding social-security information to these data obviously made sense, as well as material from the Bureau of Labor Statistics and the U.S. Civil Service Commission, which had already held dossiers on nearly everyone who had ever applied for Federal employment since 1939. Then the Census Bureau information was added and the Defense Department's military records, and finally the FBI files. Once the FBI records went into the data banks, they were soon followed by those of the house un-American Activities Committee and by the CIA. Some of the material was, of course, restricted, and available only to the proper officials.

Thus far, all these records had been Federal, but the addition of the FBI and other police files made so much sense that the local police of every state, city and town cooperated and there soon came to be a national criminal record of practically everyone in the country, even though an individual's record might consist of no more than a traffic violation.

But that had just been the beginning. Medical information was soon added. At the same time another element was utilizing the computer data banks—the universities, the libraries, the newspapers and such depositories of human knowledge. Early in the game they began cooperation in storing information. Soon there was a gigantic data bank of books, encyclopedias, newspaper morgues; everything from Einstein's works to Escoffier's Cook Book. The big step had been taken when it was decided to include the Library of Congress and, a few years later, through a special exchange arrangement with Her Majesty's Government, the British Museum Library.

Ultimately, this educational material was combined with the Federal Government's information on individual citizens and all was placed in the National Data Banks. The thing had really begun in earnest. Every newspaper, every magazine, every book and pamphlet published in the world, in every written language, was translated by computer and placed in the files, in both its original and translated forms.

Neck and neck with these developments were those in the field of banking and credit, the trend to the cashless-checkless society and the universal credit account. The computer, plus the portable pocket TV phone, made possible a national credit system eliminating money, in the old sense of the word. A person's income was put to his account. By placing his pocket transceiver on the payment screen in any store, restaurant, public transportation vehicle, or wherever, he was debited to whatever extent required.

Yes. Everything, no matter how trivial, was in the data banks. Why not? There was infinite room. The early punch cards had been replaced by magnetic tapes, and they in turn by much-improved methods of storing the information flooding into the computer banks. The *Encyclopedia Britannica* could be compressed into an area no larger than a fifty-cent piece. So why not store it all, all accumulated information?

But the thing which presently confronted Ted Swain was that there was precious little, astonishingly little, on the modern commune culture, if that was what you could call it.

He imagined that his final work should include at least one chapter on the history of the commune, to trace it to its earliest origins. The conception could be found as far back as Plato's *Republic,* More's *Utopia.* But that wasn't quite it. They were both fictional.

Nevertheless, he thought, scowling into his screen as he dialed over and over again, trying to trace out what small information was available, there were actual equivalents of the modern commune in the cooperative movements of the 19th Century, most of them based on early utopian socialism.

Yes, he could find all the information he needed for a chapter or so on the preliminaries to the modern commune movement. And he would have no trouble with the primitive communes. He was so up on that subject that he would hardly have to research it at all.

But the modern! There was practically nothing at all. No wonder Dollar had been keen for him to go ahead.

Oh, there was some material, most of it not applicable to his study, as he presently saw it; articles and pamphlets on how to organize a mobile town; how to set up a local government for it; a president, a central committee, a police and fire unit, a community mobile hospital, and so forth. They stressed the need for an adequate community of interests. There was, he noted, even an archaeological mobile town, complete with a small mobile museum. They evidently went from dig to dig, throughout North America, sometimes conducting digs of their own when they could get permission. It occurred to Ted Swain that it would be a commune after his own heart. But no; he wanted to be a professional, not an amateur.

His stomach was growling. He clicked off the TV screen, and stared ahead of him, wondering what time it was. He'd lost track of the passage of the hours. He'd been sitting there until just short of dinner, without anything in his stomach but the eggs he'd made for himself and Martha, or Marsha, or whatever the hell her name was, that morning.

Well, he didn't have time to dial the ultramarket for the ingredients to cook a decent meal now, he thought. He'd go over to the restaurant. He came to his feet, yawning and scowling. The fact was that this was not something that could be researched in the data banks. He would have to get out in the field.

Where the hell was he going to begin? There didn't even seem to be lists of the various communes. Evidently they came and went at such a pace that no record

31

could be kept. They shifted. A communard might be in a local commune in New England one day and travel down to one on the Florida peninsula the next. Or, for that matter, the whole commune might make such a move.

He made his way into the living room and toward the door. That bastard Englebrecht hadn't the foggiest notion, when he came up with this brainstorm, of what was involved. Ted had a sneaking suspicion that there were literally tens of millions of Americans now living in the many types of commune; fugitives from the ordinary way of life under this alleged utopia, the ultrawelfare society which had evolved in the past quarter century.

Tens of millions? For the first time it occurred to him that more than ninety percent of the population of United America lived by what was actually the norm, on Universal Guaranteed Income. It was from this huge number that the communes were being formed.

The community buildings of West Hurley were about a kilometer from Ted Swain's house. The inhabitants of the town valued privacy above all and their houses were not packed together. The very thought of living in a hi-rise apartment building along with several thousand others was enough to chill Ted Swain's blood.

He didn't bother to summon a car, since he never rode if he could walk. A full-time scholar could go to pot in short order if he didn't take advantage of every opportunity to exercise.

The swimming pool, the tennis courts and even the jai alai court were getting a good afternoon play. Ted waved to various acquaintances, but pushed on to the restaurant, which he found practically empty.

Mike Latimer was sitting at the bar, nursing a drink. When Ted sat down at a table, he picked up his glass and brought it over.

He said, "You know what's gone out of this world of ours?"

"No," Ted said, looking up from the menu set into the table top. "What?"

"The bartender, that's what. It used to be that a well-intentioned hard-drinking man could go into a bar and spend the afternoon telling the long-suffering bartender all his troubles. And the bartender had to listen. It was an occupational hazard. Now everything's automated." He sat down across from Ted Swain.

Ted said, "You can always talk with a friend."

"No, that's not it. You don't get the scenario. If you've got a friend you're drinking with he wants to tell you *his* troubles, not listen to yours. The old-fashioned bartender never told you his troubles, he just listened sympathetically to *your* woes."

Ted chuckled. Mike was a slight, amiable type, good-looking, dark of hair and brows and with a beautiful speaking voice. All of which fitted in with his trade. He was a TV news commentator, specializing in this immediate vicinity, local news, local gossip. His sense of humor was sparkling and he was popular. He liked his work, and since his listeners liked him, he was returned to the job time after time on work-muster day. He was one of the few in West Hurley who had employment.

Ted ran his finger down the menu and ordered a whale steak, along with suitable vegetables and a salad. He felt ravenous. He put his transceiver on the payment screen, dialed the meal, leaned back and looked thoughtfully at his tablemate.

He pulled on the lobe of his right ear, which was big enough as it was, without needing stretching, and said, "You know, it occurs to me that you're just the man I want."

Mike Latimer pretended to wince. "So you've come to that, eh? Turned queerie. Well, no thanks. I go for girls."

"Doesn't everybody know it? You've poked practically every mopsy in town. What I meant was, if anybody knew anything about the communes in this area, you would."

"Communes? What about the communes?"

"Academician Englebrecht has come up with a subject for my dissertation. He wants me to do my book on a comparison between prehistoric communes and the modern ones."

Mike looked at him questioningly. "I thought your specialty was ancient society."

"It is. This is a new departure for me. There's practically nothing in the data banks on modern communes, a fact that floors me. How can anything as big as they are currently have no data on them?"

Mike Latimer took a pull at his drink. "They're dropouts," he said. "They're misfits in this culture. Some of them are bitter about it. Some couldn't care less. But they have no intention of living like the rest of us. They want to do their own thing, not be bothered by society. So they contribute as little as possible to the statistics compiled by the data banks."

Ted Swain said, "You mean, all of them?"

"No, not all of them. West Hurley, here, is one type of commune. Less far out than most, perhaps, but a commune of single, largely young, people interested in lots of poking, lots of sports, lots of entertainment. But there aren't many real rebels among us. Actually, we're rather on the conservative side, as communes go. We cooperate with the authorities, including the National Data Banks, we vote in the civic elections, we get along with everybody. But we don't live in apartments in one of the pseudocities; we've left the cities."

Mike thought about it for a moment before adding, "I suspect that this commune thing is considerably bigger than has been let out. And I suspect that it's going to get bigger still. In a way, you might say that Robert Owen lives."

"Robert Owen?"

"Never heard of him? An early 19th Century British reformer. Father of the cooperative movement. Sort of a utopian socialist, I suppose you'd call him," Mike said.

The center of the table dropped and then returned

with Ted's meal. He took up his napkin and utensils and forked an initial bite.

He said, "I met George Dollar at Englebrecht's apartment. He was hot for the project. I got the impression that he thought the communes were getting out of hand."

Mike was surprised. "Dollar, eh? He's backing you?"

"To the extent he can, evidently. From what he said, he'd like to see more information in the National Data Banks on the communes. They don't seem to have had much luck getting information out of them."

Mike grunted. "I can see why. Suppose you wanted information on this new art colony mobile town that's shaping up over toward Saugerties. Suppose you sent a man in, pretending he was an artist, to pry around. How long do you think it would be before they knew damn well he was no artist?"

He cut a bite of the steak. It was, as always, superlative. Marsha had been right; the autochef never missed. However, he *still* had his unfounded prejudice against automated cooking.

Ted said, "Why not send in a man who was an artist?"

"Because if a man has been selected by the computers for a job in the National Data Banks, he's no artist. He's a data man and how many statisticians know one end of a paint brush from the other?"

Ted said, "Well, I'm evidently committed. So tomorrow I start checking out the communes in this vicinity. You have any ideas?"

"Yeah, don't."

Ted scowled at him. "What do you mean? Why not? It's my big chance to get my academician's degree, hombre."

"It's also your big chance to get your teeth kicked in."

Chapter Five

"What is that supposed to mean?" Ted said in irritation.

"Look," Mike said earnestly, after finishing his drink, "you're not reading the script, you don't get the scenario. These people don't want to be bothered. They don't want to be investigated by some stooge for Dollar. Sure, you won't have any difficulty in some senior-citizen's community, full of old folks who have banded together for companionship. But suppose you look into one of these youth communes where they refuse to vote, hide fugitives and all the rest of it. How do you think they'd respond to Doctor Theodore Swain prying around asking questions about everything they do?"

"Like I said, I'm afraid I'm committed," Ted grumbled. "How am I going to locate some of these people?"

Mike was unhappy with him but he said, "Probably your best bet is to get names and locations from the communes you investigate. One will tell you about others. I know of some in the near vicinity you can start with. That new art colony mobile town, New Woodstock, for instance. Then there's Lesbos, over near Kingston. It's something like West Hurley, here, only several times larger. Then there's Walden, up near Lake Bomoseen; it's an agricultural commune."

"I've heard about that one," Ted nodded. "I would have thought they'd have picked a better climate."

"They seem to like the change in season," Mike said. "There are quite a few of these agriculture communes. The back-to-nature fling. Natural foods and all. Horse and cow shit, instead of chemical fertilizer."

"I'll have to take in at least one of those," Ted nodded. "Well, tomorrow I start."

"Zoroaster knows where you'll end," Mike told him sourly. "How about an after-dinner drink?"

"Not for me, tonight," Ted told him. "Guzzle makes me sleepy and I have some thinking to do."

"You sure as hell have," Mike Latimer told him.

"Don't roach me, hombre," Ted said, coming to his feet. "See you in the future."

"I hope you have one," Mike said.

As Ted Swain left the building, he passed a handsome athletic-type girl, who was carrying a tennis racket and smelled faintly of perspiration, just entering. She was topless, which revealed that she was well-tanned, and flashed a brilliant smile revealing a set of teeth as beautiful as any Ted had ever seen. He ruefully remembered those teeth, from a past engagement. Fay was prone to bite, in climax.

"Hi, Fay, what spins?" he asked her.

"Hello, Ted. Listen, do you have anybody on tonight? Marsha's been spreading around about that Hindu—or whatever it is—position of yours."

He said, "Not tonight, sweety. Ordinarily, I'd say wizard, but I've got some things to work out. Try Mike, over there, if you need to get poked. He seems to be at loose ends."

"I like bigger men," she said. "I'll scout around." She grinned at him as she passed by into the dining room. "Hombre, it's getting tough in West Hurley when a girl's got to beg to get laid."

"Maybe things will look up later," he called after her as he turned to go.

Back at the house he made a few notes on what Mike had told him, including the names of the communes he'd known about.

He dubiously eyed the library-booster screen on his desk. He had planned to resume his investigations of earlier in the day but somehow didn't feel up to it. Tomorrow was another time; he'd pitch in then, he decided.

He went on back into his kitchen, took down a ceramic canister from one of the shelves and took off the lid. There were only two pieces of hashish fudge left. He'd have to whomp up another batch; he disliked the commercial stuff. He took up one of the pieces and ate it slowly.

Ted Swain invariably ate his cannabis, either in fudge form or marmalade, since he had never learned to smoke, or, at least, not to inhale, which was necessary for any real effect from smoking pot.

By the time he had reached his teens and had taken the required school subjects in narcotics and their affiliates, the use of tobacco had dropped off precipitously. Once the profit motive had disappeared from production and distribution, and courses for all citizens were mandatory, some of the old means of flight from reality had fallen away. Not disappeared, but dropped off. Few among the younger generations took tobacco or even alcohol, for that matter. Cannabis, after it had become legalized for all those who had passed their tests on the subject, had taken over. The hard drugs were as illegal as ever and their sources so well dried up that they were all but unknown.

Ted Swain had taken his examinations on narcotics and since then had been eligible to purchase both alcohol and cannabis. He wasn't a heavy user of either, but he enjoyed the escape both offered, occasionally.

He returned to his living room to watch the evening news broadcast that he particularly favored.

The Reunited Nations were still at their debate on whether or not there should be more consolidation of the smaller nations still remaining. Now that Interlingua was understood by literally everyone under the age of about twenty-five and most others as well, there was no reason why small islands, former tribal areas, and midget nations should not amalgamate, or possibly join one of the great political units such as United America, Common Europe, or the Soviet Complex.

At that point, Ted Swain wondered why they still called it the "Soviet Complex." It was about as Soviet, in the old sense, as Europe or the Americas. Time had marched on.

There were evidently new breakthroughs in the field of the laser moles, which were now delving as deep as five miles into the earth's crust in mining operations. Completely automated, of course; men couldn't work at that depth. Well, Swain thought, that would at least mean an end to the alarm about depletion of world resources. That and extracting minerals and other valuables from the sea.

There was a brief flash from Denver, the new national capital. Warren Edgar, Chief Director of the National Security Forces, had requested of the Civil Congress an increase of 50,000 police agents in his department.

Ted looked blankly at the screen. 50,000 more police agents? For what? So far as he could see the nation already had more than it required. He had always thought that the large number of National Security men employed was just one more make-work affair.

There were a couple of items about the moon base and Satellite City, but he was completely out of his depth and their significance escaped him.

The cannabis was beginning to get to him. He felt moderately high and decided that he had made a mistake in turning Fay down. If the girls in the community wanted to try some of the more exotic sex positions he had turned up in his researches into other cultures, who was he to say no?

He turned off the screen, took out his pocket transceiver and dialed Fay. She was sitting in the community bar, obviously just a bit tight.

Ted said, "Hi, girl. Listen, I changed my mind."

She grinned at him mockingly. "Oh, you did, eh? Wizard. But the trouble is this little mink has found another hombre, so you can just go get goosed."

"Hmmm," he said. "Okay, but you'll never learn how the Mayans did it, from whoever he is. I've got a monopoly."

"Shirk off, chum-pal," she laughed, and her face faded.

He grunted mild irritation and dialed Marsha.

Marsha was in bed and behind her, faintly, he could make out a man's head.

"Never mind," he said. "Carry on."

There were a multitude of other girls in town, of course, but he decided the hell with it and went on into his bedroom, undressed and retired. He picked up his bedroom library booster from the nightstand and dialed the day's book reviews. He scanned the novels and decided on one set in Peru, some sort of an exploration-suspense story.

In the morning, following the usual routine of his toilet and then breakfast, he had to face up to it. If he was going to follow through on this project he had to get going. Possibly Englebrecht had been right; somebody else might beat him to publication. With so little material available on the communes, it was just a matter of time until writers, both scholars and otherwise, began to fill the void.

He looked down at the few notes on his desk and grimaced. He hardly knew where to begin. Well, one thing was sure: if some of these groups were as touchy as Mike Latimer had said, he wasn't going to be able to sit around taking notes in full view.

He went back into the kitchen-dining room and to his order box and dialed the ultramarket in the community buildings. He dialed information and said, "Is there available a minirecorder of a type that can be hidden in one's clothing, and the material recorded, beamed back to one's home?"

A metallic voice said, "We do not have this item in

stock but can secure one from the warehouses in Kingston within ten minutes, sir."

"Please do," Ted said. He put his pocket transceiver on the payment screen to have the amount involved deducted from his credit balance.

That brought to mind the fact that he would probably be incurring more than usual expenses during the following weeks. He said into the screen, "Credit balance please, of S-204-121645M."

The screen said, "Three thousand and forty-two pseudodollars and fifty-four cents."

Well, that should be more than ample, especially since there was a quarterly payment of his Universal Guaranteed Income due to him in less than a month. Ted Swain seldom used up the full amount of his income. In fact, few did. When you didn't, your balance reverted to the nation; there was no such thing as letting it accumulate or leaving it to someone in a will. Ostentatious spending was largely a thing of the past. Not completely, but largely. At long last the country had achieved the point where it could produce an abundance for all. With it had dropped away the old keeping-up-with-the-Joneses disease. No one bothered to attempt to surpass his neighbor's possessions.

While waiting for the electronic bug to arrive, he went into the bath. He threw his underwear, socks and the Yucatan shirt into the disposal chute, then went back into the kitchen-dining room and dialed himself fresh clothing from the ultramarket, after putting his transceiver on the payment screen. It was delivered immediately and by the time he had donned it the minirecorder equipment had arrived in the vacuum-tube delivery box.

He opened the container and took the device and its directions back into his study. He sat down and read the instructions. It was simple enough. The bug itself was tiny and had a pin with it which you could stick in some out-of-the-way part of your clothing. Just about any place would do, evidently. You left the recording box sitting right on your desk, or wherever else you wanted to put it. When you wished to record, you activated the bug and what it picked up was beamed to the disk in the recording box.

Very simple indeed. He tried it a few times, just to be sure, and was pleased with the excellent reception. He wiped the disk, on which he had been recording, and pinned the bug on the inner side of his jacket lapel.

All set to go. He dialed himself a two-seater electrosteamer and, while he waited for it, left a message on his TV phone. "I've gone away for a time to do some research on a new project and haven't the vaguest idea of when I'll be back." Actually, of course, anyone who wanted him badly enough could always find him on their pocket transceiver.

He headed for his front door and left a message on the identity screen there for potential visitors. "I'm gone, for how long I don't know, to do some research."

The car came buzzing up to the curb and he went down to it. It was a near duplicate of the one he'd had the day before, with the exception that this one had a top. He had no idea whether or not he might run into rain before he returned.

He took the road map from the glove compartment and traced his finger around the area. Yes, there was the community that Mike had mentioned, Lesbos, near Kingston. He could stop there first and if the visit wasn't productive go on over to Saugerties where he had heard the new mobile town art colony was being assembled.

He started up and headed out of West Hurley, keeping to the surface roads. He was in no hurry and enjoyed the countryside. Below ground, it was as though you were in an endless tunnel. Well-ventilated and illuminated, true, but with absolutely nothing to see. The best you could do was switch on the TV set.

Ted Swain could remember back to the days before the below-surface expressways had been completed. The superhighways and freeways of that time had been packed and possibly four vehicles out of every five were involved in commercial purpose. There were

42

plenty of trucks and buses, but even most of the cars contained passengers with little or no interest in the scenery. A man going to his job, a salesman, a housewife going to the supermarket. They couldn't care less about the view.

Today, such traffic stuck to the underground. Somebody who wished to enjoy the countryside drove on the surface. And the reforesting and antipollution measures were restoring this part of America to a condition similar to what it had been like a century before. The vicinity wasn't really suited to modern agriculture and was being returned to living areas and what amounted to an enormous national park. There were towns and even smaller communities, and isolated houses as well for those who preferred them, but what industry prevailed was as underground as the expressways, and well away from the eye of the pedestrian, cyclist or motorist.

The road dipped and turned, having been laid out with a view toward beauty rather than speed. It had been one of the most monumental tasks of the new society to destroy the freeways of the mid-20th Century and restore the surface of the nation to the acceptable, enjoyable country it had been before the coming of the first and second industrial revolutions.

Mike Latimer had been right about the size of Lesbos. It seemed to be approximately twice that of West Hurley. Ted was moderately surprised that he had never heard of the place before. But then, with the exodus from the pseudocities into the countryside, literally thousands of new small towns and communities had sprung up in such desirable areas as this.

In many respects this community was similar to the one in which he lived. There were few people on the streets and no children whatsoever. Another commune which banned them, as did West Hurley, he imagined. The houses were set a bit closer together, perhaps, and the community buildings were more extensive, but that was to be expected in view of the larger population. And evidently Lesbos was prospering; quite a few new

43

structures were going up. Ted noted that the Construction Guild was becoming even more ultramated. Two men, or women, seemed all that were currently necessary to supervise the machines that put up a house. And it would appear that an hour or so was about the time required.

The community buildings were set on the edge of town, rather than in its center, as in West Hurley, and he noted that they had a nine-hole golf course. He wondered how long it would be before the West Hurley residents would get around to that. His community had quite a few golfers, though he wasn't one himself.

He left his electrosteamer in the parking area, without dismissing it, and headed for what appeared to be an administration building. There would probably be some sort of official there. With a town this size, hundreds of houses, they'd probably have someone on full time. No matter how automated you could make policing, waste collection, street maintenance and so forth, there was still need for human activity in running a community.

A girl came out through the door as he was about to enter.

Ted said, "I beg your pardon, Miss. Is there some sort of town official I could talk to?"

Her eyebrows went up. She was a feminine little thing, done up with considerably more frills than Swain was accustomed to in West Hurley. In his own town young women were inclined to sports and dressed accordingly.

She said, "Gloria is in the office that leads off to the right, just as you enter."

"Wizard," he said and looked after her as she tripped on down the walk. She was so feminine that she appeared artificial. He shrugged, turned and entered.

A woman who evidently was Gloria, was seated at a desk in a small efficiency office. The only other occupant of the room sat at another desk, behind an autosecretary. She, too, seemed on the ultrafeminine side.

But not Gloria. In fact, Ted Swain had to look twice to realize that it was Gloria, rather than, say, George. Gloria was one big hunk of woman, built like a lumberjack and more or less looking like one, not to speak of dressing the part.

She rasped, and her voice went along with her appearance, "What can I do for you?" Her tone indicated that she wasn't desperately interested in the answer. In fact, she seemed to have a chip on her shoulder.

Ted said hesitantly, and wishing that he had rehearsed this a bit, "I . . . I've been considering joining a commune and am out looking around. You know, casing the different ones, seeing if I could find one that seemed to be compatible."

She came to her feet and strode around the desk and confronted him, her face in fury.

"What kind of flat are you?"

The girl behind the autosecretary giggled in a high voice.

Ted was flabbergasted. "What did I say?"

Her hands were on her hips, but suddenly one of them lashed out, in a fist, and caught him flush on the right eye. She moved in fast, both hands pounding.

"Hey, for Christ's sakes!" he blurted. "Take it easy!"

"You funker! Get spayed!" she shouted, slugging him as fast as she could operate.

Ted fell back, holding up his hands to ward her off.

"What in the hell goes on here?" he yelped.

Chapter Six

He grabbed her desperately, pinning her arms to the sides of her body. Furious as she was, he outweighed her by at least twenty pounds and in his undergraduate days Ted Swain had been a member of the university wrestling team.

"Let go of me, you bastard!" she yelled.

Behind her, the secretary, or whatever she was, said shrilly, "Knee him, Gloria!"

But Gloria had already thought of that and tried to.

Ted Swain turned sideways. He shook her as brutally as he could, considering their position.

"What in the hell is the matter with you people?" he shouted. "Have you gone completely drivel-happy? What did I say?"

He pushed her away from him and took several steps backward and held up his hands as though in surrender.

Gloria at first began to lunge forward, but then came to a halt and glared at him. She was panting in her fury.

She spat out, finally, "What's spinning with you, you funker?"

He made a gesture of despair, knocking his fist against his forehead to show his complete incomprehension. "All I did was say I was interested in joining a

46

commune and Lesbos is one of the places I thought I'd check out."

"Oh, you did, huh?" Her hands were on her hips again. She glared at him suspiciously, but then she snapped, "Lesbos, Lesbos. Doesn't that mean anything to you?"

He looked at her blankly. "The original is an island off Greece, isn't it?"

"Yes, damn it. And what's it famous for?"

All of a sudden he felt like an ass. "The home of the poetess Sappho," he said. "You mean the theme of this commune . . ."

"Yes, you silly flat. Have you seen any men in this town?"

"Well, no. Except a couple working on the erection of those new houses."

"We can't keep them out. The Construction Guild decides who supervises the erection of houses."

She seemed slightly mollified, evidently accepting the fact that he had been sincere and not deliberately trying to provoke her. She turned, rounded her desk and sat down.

The other girl giggled again and without turning Gloria snapped at her, "Shut up, Phyllis."

"Yes, dear," Phyllis said contritely.

Ted was staring at the two of them. "You mean this whole town? I mean . . . your, uh, theme . . . uh . . ."

She snapped, "You think we're ashamed of it? The theme of this commune is Sapphic love. No men are allowed. If you're gay, why don't you get on down to New Tangier?"

He looked at her blankly. "Where?"

"New Tangier. Down near Princeton University City. There must be at least two thousand of you boys there. Gay as a mardi gras."

"Two thousand," he said. "You mean two thousand . . ."

"Queer as chicken shit," she said. "I can't stand the sight of them myself. But possibly you . . ."

He shook his head. "No. I'm, ah, queer for girls, myself."

The secretary giggled.

Gloria said, "Shut up, Phyllis."

"Yes, dear."

Gloria was calmer, although she still didn't invite him to be seated. She said, "Why don't you try Gomorrah?"

"That's a good question," Ted said. "What's Gomorrah?"

She leered at him. "Anything goes. Gomorrah, Gomorrah. Don't you know your bible? Sodom and Gomorrah?"

"Oh," he said. "Yes, of course. You know, I've always wondered what they did in Gomorrah."

"In this Gomorrah they do everything. Too far out for me. I'm conservative."

Phyllis giggled.

Gloria said, "They're bisexual. They'll do anything with anybody. Hell, they'll do anything with anything. So don't take your dog along, unless he's used to that sort of tail." She snorted lewdly.

Suddenly he was tired of the bent of the conversation. He said, "Sorry to have intruded on you, and to have misconstrued." He began to turn to leave.

"That's all right," Gloria said gruffly. "But now, get going. We're here in Lesbos to get away from you chauvinistic males and we don't like you coming around roaching us."

He couldn't keep from looking over at Phyllis. "What a waste," he muttered.

"Shirk off," she sneered.

He returned to the car, noting now what he hadn't before: all the people on the streets were female. They were of varying ages, but all female, if you could call a lesbian "female." Most were dressed in one of two extremes, either much in the masculine tradition or in the same overly feminine manner of Phyllis and the girl from whom he had asked directions.

He got back into the car, took a deep breath and

shook his head. "Some commune," he muttered, starting up the vehicle. "Well, it's all recorded. It should make a paragraph or so in the dissertation. Wonder how many more of this type are scattered around the country?"

As he drove in the direction of Saugerties, he thought it over and decided it made quite a bit of sense, given the homosexual viewpoint. In the old days they had largely been pariahs, forced to disguise their sexual tastes or suffer the scorn or amusement of their fellow citizens, at best, and actual physical danger or even imprisonment, at worst. In fact, he had read somewhere that in some of the states in the old America homosexuality was a capital offense. Under the Revised Constitution homosexuality was legal between consenting adults, and Lesbos, evidently, was the ultimate result. Lesbians banded together into their own commune and led what was for them a normal life. The same applied to male homosexuals, it seemed.

What was the name of the town she had mentioned? New Tangier, and it was down near Princeton. It came to him, somewhat unhappily, that he should probably investigate the place. Possibly he wouldn't receive quite as violent a reception as he had in Lesbos. But, on the other hand, suppose they tried to convert him? He snorted in amusement. Hell, suppose they tried to rape him? Some opinions to the contrary, homosexuals were not necessarily fluttery effeminates. They could be as rough and tough as the next man.

But now that he had communes with sexual themes on his mind, what other possibilities were there? Of course, the word "homosexual" was rather all-embracing and possibly some of such communes might be variations on the norm, whatever the norm could be. But perhaps New Tangier might be populated by practitioners of sodomy; another commune devoted to fellatio.

Now that he thought about it, he realized that a whole book, certainly a pamphlet, could be devoted to these communes with sexual themes.

49

What else? Could there be a commune settled by sadists and masochists? They could work out their woes on each other. That would be something to see. He grunted. Carry it still further. How about a commune devoted to nymphomania and satyrism? He had to chuckle at the picture invoked but, in actuality, it might make some sense at that.

He began to see some of the reasons why George Dollar was anxious to get more material on the communes into his data banks. Why, whole new ways of life were developing in them. Who had ever heard of complete towns composed of nothing but practicing lesbians? He couldn't think of another example in history. Oh, there had been a great deal of homosexuality among the ancient Greeks—but not whole communities of them.

Although he had never seen it, he understood that there was one of the new king-size camping-ground sites just to the west of the city of Saugerties. They were a phenomenon to be found all over North America now, and the larger ones could accommodate thousands of campers, trailers and mobile homes. He didn't have any difficulty locating this one.

He stopped at the entry and said into the autoreceptionist there, "Where would I find New Woodstock?"

The metallic voice said, "Their auxiliary and administrative units are parked at the corner of D and Tenth Streets."

It wasn't hard to work out the layout of the grounds. There were signs at every corner, to help out. And there was a sign before the mobile town which he was seeking. NEW WOODSTOCK, in large letters, and, beneath, *Mobile Art Colony*.

He parked and made his way over.

There was a small boy playing on the lawn before the largest of what were evidently the town's administration buildings. He had a toy electrosteamer truck which he was able to send scooting about the area with a remote control apparatus which seemed complicated although the child was having no difficulty whatsoever.

Ted Swain stopped before him and said, "Sonny, where would I find one of the town officials?"

The truck rolled over his right foot. It was surprisingly heavy and he winced.

The boy said, "My name isn't Sonny, it's Timmy."

"Oh, sorry, Timmy. My name's Ted."

"You an artist?" the boy said.

"No. No, I'm not."

"Then you can't join up with New Woodstock."

Ted Swain took in air. "I wasn't planning to."

"You're not allowed, unless you're an artist. My dad's an artist. And I'm going to be one when I grow up."

"All right, wizard. But where would I find one of New Woodstock's officials?"

"Maybe you better see the town cop." The boy pointed. "Over there."

Over there was a mobile home of moderate size, compared to the others in the vicinity. Before it was parked what looked to Ted Swain like a converted police vehicle of the type that patrolled the automated expressways.

He said his thanks and made his way in that direction.

New Woodstock, it seemed, had no taboos against children such as applied in both West Hurley and Lesbos. It came to him that there must be a good many communes these days that barred kids, communities of older people who would be irritated by their noise, communes of all the various types of homosexuals, communes of unmarrieds, such as his own, and communes of people who simply didn't like children. He wondered if the taboo were spreading. He'd have to consider that in his dissertation.

Before he had quite reached the trailer, the door opened and a man stepped out. He was moderately tall, with a military carriage. His hair was wiry, his complexion dark and his features so heavy that he would hardly have been considered handsome by average American standards. He wore a khaki semiuniform.

He said to Ted, "Something I can do for you?"

"You're the, uh, local representative of National Security?"

The other shook his head. "No. We have no full-time National Security officer. I'm unofficial. All town officials here are elected, all work voluntarily. Nothing in it but the honor."

"Oh, I see." In view of his experience in Lesbos, Ted Swain decided on a different approach. He said carefully, "The fact is, I'm doing a book on the communes. I'm looking for material on at least one of the mobile towns. I thought perhaps you'd let me ask a few questions."

The other scowled slightly and chewed his heavy lower lip. Ted Swain estimated that he was at least one quarter African. Evidently there were no racial barriers in the mobile art colony. Which brought to mind the fact that there was an aspect into which he'd have to look. Were there communes of Blacks, communes of Orientals, Jews, communes of Spanish-Americans, Amerinds, and so forth and so on? There must be. How was he going to be able to investigate such? They'd surely have chips on their shoulders.

The town's unofficial policeman said, "What kind of questions?"

Ted had to laugh in self-deprecation. "Actually, I don't know. I'll have to play it by ear. I don't know the first thing about mobile towns, not to speak of a mobile art colony. I suppose my best bet would be to just sit down with you and let you talk. Maybe some questions will come to mind."

"You're not a government man, snooping?"

Ted shook his head. "My name's Swain. Doctor Theodore Swain. I'm studying over at the university city. Ethnology. You can check my identification."

"It won't be necessary." The other held out a hand. "My name's Bat Hardin."

They shook and Hardin turned as he said, "Come on in and sit down. Are you cleared for drinking?"

"Of course." Ted followed him into the trailer.

He had never been inside of one before. Had never had occasion. He looked around curiously. It was a miracle of compactness. About the size of a miniapartment in a pseudocity, it was composed of bedroom, bath, kitchen and living room, and seemingly had all of the amenities boasted by his own more ample home. He noticed a TV screen, a library booster, a refrigerator, an autobar, an electric stove, even a vocotyper on a small desk.

His host went over to the autobar, saying over his shoulder, "Sit down. You've never been in a trailer before, have you? What'll you have? I've got this bar set up with rum, gin, vodka, brandy, whiskey, both scotch and bourbon, coke, gingerale, tonic, and soda. Not as wide a selection as if I were permanent, but sufficient."

"No, I've never been in a mobile home before," Ted said, seating himself on a comfortable couch. "Rum and coke would be fine."

Hardin dialed, waited, and in a moment the top of the bar sank in to return with two long cold glasses. He picked them up, handed one to Ted, and seated himself in an easy chair across from his guest.

Swain held up his glass in a toast. "Cheers, cheers," he said.

"Cheers, cheers." Bat Hardin took a sip and said, "Now, where do we begin?"

Ted Swain was rueful. "Like I say, I don't know. This assignment was thrown at me out of a clear sky. I've never had any particular interest in the commune movement, though, as has been pointed out to me, I suppose I live in one myself. You would call New Woodstock a commune, wouldn't you?"

Bat Hardin thought about it. "I guess so. The term is elastic. I suppose that the spirit of Robert Owen still lives."

Ted Swain frowned. "Owen, Owen? Seems to me I just heard his name recently. Some British reformer."

"Ummm. Quite an idealist. Well, let's see what I can tell you about mobile towns. Actually, I imagine the germ was there almost as soon as the development of the automobile. Trailers really made the scene as far back as the 1920s. By the 1930s and 40s, permanent towns of them began to appear. During the Second World War, with the fantastic housing shortages that developed around the newly built war industries, they came into their own with a vengeance. Trailers could be mass produced, and were."

"But mobile towns?" Ted Swain said.

"They really began in a small way not long after the Second World War. Groups of trailer owners would form clubs and take off for extended vacations. They weren't really towns, of course. By that time there were literally multitudes of trailer parks and some of them held thousands of trailers and large mobile homes that weren't really expected to be moved. Usually, the wheels were even removed, the houses propped up. By then some fifteen percent of all the homes constructed in America were mobile."

Ted said, "Why would anyone prefer to live in a trailer rather than a house?"

"At that time, largely for the cheap living. They were tax free and comparatively simple to maintain."

"But these weren't mobile towns. The residents of these trailer parks didn't go and come en masse, did they?"

"Well, no. That really got going with the advent of Universal Guaranteed Income, in the 1970s. All of a sudden, somebody on relief, as they called it then, didn't have to remain in New York, Chicago, Los Angeles, or one of the other large cities, in order to collect. They could go anywhere. Relief became Federal rather than local. Obviously, nobody in their right mind wants to live in a place like Harlem or Watts must have been. They took off from the cities like lemmings. Some settled down in smaller communities in desirable parts of the country, but some took to wheels. Those that liked the nomadic life soon saw the advantages of banding together. In a group of as small as twenty or thirty, you'd find that one was a TV repairman, one a car mechanic, another a doctor or nurse, another a schoolteacher, and so on. After a while the mobile communities would get large enough to pool their resources and buy an auxiliary or two."

"What's this auxiliary razzle?"

"Well, for example, we plan eventually to number about five hundred homes. We'll have a mobile hospital, a school, an administration building, an electronics repair shop, a repair garage, even a mobile store. Town members who have more than one driver in their family will take turns driving them when we're under way."

Ted Swain considered it. "Where do you get these auxiliary trailers?"

"The same place we get our homes. We rent them from the National Production Congress. We have a community fund. It's no strain. These mobile towns are cheap to live in. Hardly ever do we use up all of our credit."

Ted was fascinated. He looked about the interior of the compact trailer. "I notice that yours is smaller than some of the others. Why would that be?"

The other shrugged. "Comfort and convenience. Some of the families will have several children. They need more bedrooms, more elbow room. Sometimes they'll have two units that have to be pulled separately when under way, but hook together when camped."

Ted said, "Tell me, where do you plan to go when your town is completely assembled?"

"Down the Pan-American Highway to South America, taking our time, stopping where we wish and staying for as long a period as we want at each stop."

Ted frowned at him. He said, "But those of your members who work, how will they get back and forth to the job? Certainly a vacation wouldn't last that long."

"That's it," Bat Hardin said. "None of us work. We're all on Universal Guaranteed Income."

"All five hundred homes?" Ted Swain was incredulous. "Nobody at all has been taken on job-muster day?"

"That's right," Hardin said, his voice even. "Most of us, though not all, are artists of one type or another. Painters, sculptors, writers, ceramists, even one composer. The rest of us are attracted to the arts, and possibly the so-called Bohemian life. We wouldn't want to take a job even if we were selected on muster day."

Chapter Seven

Ted Swain said, "Well, suppose your town was underway, on this trip, down in, say, Panama, and muster day came and a couple of your people were selected. They'd have to come back and take the job."

Bat Hardin looked at him. "No, they wouldn't. You see, we're *really* a commune. We pool our resources. Everybody's income goes into the kitty. If somebody is unfortunate enough to lose their rights to the Universal Guaranteed Income, it doesn't make any difference. With five hundred homes, most of them with more than one inhabitant, we can afford to carry a few dropouts. But that's one of the reasons we don't like National Security officers, or snoopers from the National Data Banks, coming around. Theoretically, it's illegal not to respond to a muster-day call, if the computers select you for a job."

"Look here," Ted said. "I don't want to roach you. It's none of my business. But this is an aspect of the communes and that's what I'm trying to find out about. Now, the way I see it, man has finally gotten to the point where he can apply that old adage, 'from each according to his abilities, to each according to his needs.' Who was it who first said that, Marx?"

"Search me," Hardin said. "Go on."

"The thing is that so little labor is needed now that most of us haven't the chance to hold down a job. We're simply not needed. We get our Universal Guaranteed Income, whether we work or not, and nobody gets any more than anyone else. However, I think we owe it to our society to respond if and when we are called on job-muster day. Don't you?"

"Not necessarily."

"Why not?" Ted demanded.

"Let those work in production and distribution who want to. This community isn't composed of a group of loafers. It's an art colony. Creation of art is work. It's usually a damn sight harder work than tending some machine in an automated factory. Under the present socio-economic set-up there is no artist's guild, and for good reason. One thing a computer can't come up with, in delving into the Ability Quotient needed for some job, is figuring out the ability of an artist, a writer, a sculptor. So an artist, of whatever type, gets his Universal Guaranteed Income, along with everyone else, and is free to do his thing as best he can."

"Who decides if he's an artist or not?"

"He does, just as he has all down through history. The artist does his work because he has to. If his fellow man doesn't like the end product, it's too bad, but he keeps doing his thing."

The unofficial town cop got up, refreshed their drinks and returned with them.

Ted Swain said doggedly, "I'm in rebellion because I can't get a job. I'm ashamed to take my Universal Guaranteed Income. But here you are saying that this whole commune wouldn't do their share, even if requested."

"You're doing your share," Hardin said reasonably. "You're trying to work. So are all the artists in New Woodstock. It's just that the human race has gotten to the point where practically no work is necessary to produce plenty."

He leaned forward and for a moment stared down at the back of his hands as he worked it out. "Look at it

58

this way, Swain. Take an ultramated textile-factory today. Two or three men on a shift supervise the machinery. Seemingly, they produce, say, a hundred thousand pairs of men's pants a day. In actuality, however, it isn't they who are doing the producing. It's thousands of generations of human beings whose accumulated efforts have come down to us through the centuries. Somebody had to invent fire, develop metals, agriculture, invent the wheel, develop the sciences. Each generation added its mite and passed on its accumulated knowledge to the next generation. This is a common heritage among all human beings. Working alone, those two or three supervisors couldn't produce more than, say, half a dozen pairs of pants a day. It took the whole human race contributing down through the centuries to build that ultramated factory, so it's perfectly right that the whole country profit by it, rather than just the three men who have been selected for their jobs."

"I never thought of it that way," Ted admitted.

Bat Hardin came to his feet. "Finish your drink," he said, "and I'll show you around the town."

Ted Swain did as he was told and they stepped outside.

Bat Hardin pointed out a monstrously large vehicle, or, rather, combination of vehicles. He said, "That's the town hospital. I suppose 'clinic' would be the better word. For any major operations or other complications we have to resort to the medical facilities in whatever city or town we're parked near. When we're on the road it moves in two sections, pulled by two heavy electrosteamer trucks. When we're parked, the trucks can double as ambulances. When it's set up, as it is now, it consists of two floors, sporting twelve compartments in all. That includes the living quarters of both the doctor and nurse."

"You have a full-time doctor?"

"We will have. He hasn't turned up yet."

"The Health Guild appoints one willing to move around with you?"

"No. Not in this case. Some mobile towns have regular doctors from the guild, but we're using one that another mobile town bounced from his position as a physician. Voluntary work, of course. Just as I'm voluntary and not a member of National Security."

Ted Swain was surprised. "The Health Guild allows that? It would be something like practicing without a license."

Bat Hardin looked at him wryly. "They possibly don't know about it. I told you we didn't like the authorities snooping around. We want to be as independent and as inconspicuous as possible. An art colony doesn't like regimentation."

"It's hard to escape in modern society."

"That it is."

They strolled on past the hospital and Bat Hardin pointed out another large vehicle. "That's the administration building. Contains a board room for the executive committee, several offices and the files pertaining to the town. Makes for more work, not simply filing the material into the National Data Banks, but we like it that way. To the extent possible we keep our business to ourselves."

"Executive committee?" Ted said.

"That's right. We have precious few rules in New Woodstock, but there are some. We elect an executive committee of six members. I sit in on their meetings and have a voice, but no vote. Each week they rotate the office of senior member, something like a major."

"What happens if you have some sort of razzle between two members of the town?"

"It's brought before the executive committee and they decide. If the one ruled against doesn't accept the decision, he can appeal it to the town assembly, which consists of all adult members of New Woodstock."

"What happens if he still doesn't accept the ruling?"

Bat looked at him. "We have no mobile town jail, if that's what you were wondering about. We have only one punishment we can mete out to anyone who doesn't conform to our few regulations. He's expelled from the town."

Ted Swain was intrigued by it all. He said, "What's that complex? It looks like the largest of them all."

"It is. It travels in three sections when we're underway. It's the community store. Of course, when we're parked in a regular parking site, such as this, we use the site's ultramarket. But sometimes we're parked out in the open, or on one of the smaller sites where there are few facilities, and we have to take our own supplies along with us."

He pointed out some smaller trailers. "Repair trailers. Electronics, garage, trailer maintenance, and miscellaneous repairs."

"And you have mechanics for all those?"

"Oh, yes. Several for each category. All voluntary work, of course. They spread it around. If any major troubles develop we have to depend upon the appropriate guilds in whatever city or town we're near, but on the road we can take care of just about anything. You see, even artists often have training in some line besides the particular art they specialized in."

Ted looked over at the other as they walked. "And all the mobile towns operate like this?"

"Each differs somewhat. Some are larger, some smaller. I was with one for a while that was completely devoted to hedonism. Almost a thousand mobile homes. Two of the auxiliaries were mobile nightclubs. Operated something like an old-time circus, with big tents. Dancing and everything. We'd move south for the beaches in the winter, north for the summers. We were on one continuous party. Consumed enough guzzle and pot to keep an army high."

Ted shook his head at that one. "Why'd you leave? Sounds like a bachelor's dream."

Bat Hardin shrugged it away. "For me a party is an occasional thing. Something you enjoy, possibly, once every week or so. When it's all one continuous party, it goes stale. I wanted to do something more meaningful.

61

I'm not an artist myself, but here I can contribute to the community. Here I'm needed."

They came up to a girl seated in a folding chair before one of the mobile homes. An easel stood before her. She had several tubes of paint on a little stand next to her and was dabbing directly from them onto her canvas, without using brushes.

She was a handsome woman in the tradition of Marlene Dietrich, of yesteryear, but she wasn't living up to her potential. Obviously, she didn't give a damn about her appearance. She wore no make-up whatsoever, and there was a dab of green paint on one cheek, as though she had touched it absentmindedly. She wore nothing except a pair of paint-spattered shorts. Her breasts, which Ted Swain couldn't help noticing, were magnificent.

She looked up at their approach and said, "Hi, Bat. What spins?" She looked questioningly at Ted. "Did anybody ever tell you you look like the young Abraham Lincoln?"

Ted said, "Yes."

The town policeman said, "Sue Benny, this is Ted Swain. I'm showing him around New Woodstock. Sue Benny Voss."

She put down her paint tubes, stood and shook hands in a manly fashion. With a cock of her head she indicated the painting on which she had been working.

"What do you think of it?"

Bat laughed. "What would you expect me to think of it?"

"Get spayed, you funker." She looked at Ted. "Well?"

He said uncomfortably, "Frankly, I'm not up on modern art."

She said, "You're supposed to say it's interesting."

"You are?" He looked at it again. It was a blaze of color but he could find nothing to hang onto. "Why?"

"That's what you say when you see a painting that you either don't like or don't understand. It's part of the gobbledygook terminology of the artist world."

She looked back at it distastefully. "Maybe I should have learned to play a violin, like my dear old mother wanted."

She grimaced. "Actually, I'm trying a new technique. I don't think it's coming off."

A teenage boy came up and said, "Mr. Hardin, Ferd Zogbaum is looking for you."

The town officer said, "Oh, he is? Thanks, Johnny." He turned to Ted Swain. "I'll have to call it off, Doctor Swain. Were there any other questions?"

"Why, I don't know. Oh, one thing: do you know of any other communes in the vicinity? Particularly any that have more far-out, uh, themes?"

The other thought for a minute. "There's quite a few of them spotted around, and more forming every week, but I can't think of any particularly exotic. Let's see, there's Nature, over toward Phoenecia. Pretty sizable place. A nudist commune."

"Nudist? You mean a mobile nudist colony?"

Both the girl and Hardin laughed.

Hardin said, "Well, no. Though I guess there would be no law against it. However, I just can't picture a mobile town driving down the road in the buff. It's permanent. When anybody leaves the commune grounds, to go to work, or whatever, they put on clothes. But all the time they're on the grounds they remain nude. All for the sake of health, I suppose."

He shook hands with Ted and said, "If anything else occurs to you, drop by again. Oh, by the way, you realize, of course, that some of the things I've told you are on the confidential side. I'd appreciate it if you used discretion with such."

"Of course," Ted said.

Bat Hardin turned and left, accompanied by the boy.

Sue Benny Voss was eyeing Ted curiously. She said, "What are you looking for?"

"I'm gathering material for a dissertation on the differences between modern and primitive communes."

"What's a dissertation?"

"A book. You have to write a book on some new

subject, some contribution to learning, before you can take your academician's degree at the university."

"Oh," she said. She capped her tubes of paint. "Come on inside and have a drink. I have to take a break to allow this paint to dry, anyway."

"Wizard," he said, following her into the trailer.

After the neatness of Bat Hardin's home, her place was chaos. There were paintings and tubes of paint, there were brushes and tins of turpentine, there were paint-spattered rags and towels. There was feminine clothing scattered over the furniture, half-consumed cigarettes in overflowing ashtrays. There were several glasses, here and there, some of them with the dregs of drinks.

Sue Benny said, "Bloody mess, eh? Here, wait until I clean off a chair." She picked up the clothing from one of the chairs and stuffed it into the bottom of a closet, rather than hanging it up.

Ted said, "It looks very . . . interesting."

She laughed. "You're learning. What'll you have in the way of guzzle?"

"I've been drinking rum and coke," he said, sinking into the chair.

"Coming up," she said. And then, "Damn it, I seem to be out of rum. I'll have to get one of the boys to buy me a new supply over at the ultramarket."

"Bourbon will do," he said. "How do you mean, 'one of the boys'?"

She came back with the drinks and handed his to him. "I don't have any credit, so when I need something I have to ask someone else to buy it for me. Ultimately, it all comes out of the community funds."

He looked at her. "Oh, are you one of the town members who's refused to accept an offered job and has had her Universal Guaranteed Income discontinued?"

She took a chair across from him and crossed her legs, and very good legs they were. "Nope, not this mopsy. I'm just not eligible."

"Well, why not?"

"I'm not an American. My people came over quite a

64

while ago, from Common Europe. They thought they had enough money to last indefinitely and didn't bother to become citizens. Pop didn't know his ass from his eyebrow when it came to money matters and he managed to lose it all. That was just about when this new Universal Guaranteed Income deal came in and obviously everybody in the world, for all practical purposes, would have liked to become an American citizen to get in on the gravy train. So the government cracked down. No more new citizens, except on rare occasions. So I'm not a citizen, not eligible for the Universal Guaranteed Income."

He said, "Zoroaster! What a spot to be in. But if you're a citizen of Common Europe, why don't you go back there? They have much the same set-up now."

"I like it here. I was raised in America."

"But how'd you make a go of it before you came to New Woodstock, where they're willing to take you in?"

She shrugged her shapely shoulders, jiggling full breasts in the doing. "When I was younger I had an aunt and uncle who were citizens and they supported me. Later, I'd usually tie up with some man who'd take care of me in return for use of my fair body. Theoretically, we don't have whores anymore, but in actuality, if a girl's in a spot where she has to put out to eat, she puts out—and to just about anybody. Look, if you don't stop staring at my titties, I'm going to put a sweater on."

Chapter Eight

"Sorry," Ted said. "They're very attractive."

"See here," she said accusingly, "you want to poke me, don't you?"

"Of course," he said. "How did you know?"

"I could tell by the expression on your kilts," she said sarcastically. "All right. I always did have a weakness for Abraham Lincoln. He was the ugliest man who ever lived and possibly the most beautiful, with that infinite sadness in his expression."

"Hey," Ted complained, "I'm not quite as ugly as Old Abe."

"Damn near it. What do you say we have something to eat first? I'm starved."

"All right with me. Should I go over to the camping site's ultramarket and get something?"

She stood and went over to her small kitchen. "Not necessary. I've got some stuff here." She bent and fished in her refrigerator-freezer. "Chili con carne do?"

The gourmet in him winced but he said, "Wizard."

She brought forth two individual container-dishes and put them into the electronic heater and watched as the container top melted, becoming part of the prepared contents. The chili con carne heated but the dishes remained at room temperature. She brought them back and put them on the small table in the living room. Ted Swain had never before seen food presented this way, but he had heard of it. Evidently the mobile towns had developed needs of their own.

She got utensils from a drawer and a box of crackers from a cupboard and brought them into the living room. "Beer?" she said.

"Wizard."

She fished two plastic beer containers from the refrigerator and handed him one, then took her place across from him.

He looked at the beer. "I've never seen a container like this."

She nodded brightly. "They're especially made for travelers. In the old days, somebody having a beer as he drove along would toss the cans out on the roadside. After a few decades of this the country was ass-deep in rusty beer cans. The aluminum ones were even worse; they didn't rust. The disposable plastic ones were just as bad; they'd last forever. It took years to clean up all that clutter."

Ted Swain took a bite of the chili con carne, which turned out to be not too bad.

"So now?" he said.

"So now they still throw their empty beer containers out the window. But this is plastic with a difference. A couple of days in the sun or rain and the container melts away." She took a sip appreciatively.

They finished their chili and she took up the dish it had come in and began to eat that too. Ted Swain blinked at her.

She noticed his surprise and laughed and said, "Dessert. There's evidently a lot of things developed for the mobile towns that you flats who live in pseudocities or permanent communities have never heard of."

He took a cautious bite of his own dish. Sort of a strange combination of fruit-flavored gelatin and a very hard pie crust, almost like hardtack. It wasn't too bad actually.

"Saves a lot of space when you're underway and

can't get to the ultramarkets very easily," she explained.

"I'll bet it does." He switched subjects. "Look, Sue Benny, isn't there some manner in which you could realize some income from your paintings?"

She looked at him and twisted her expressive mouth. "How, for Christ's sake?"

"Well, I don't know anything about modern art. I'm an ethnologist. I specialize in the past. But surely . . ."

"What's an ethnologist?"

He told her.

She took their utensils, washed them quickly in the tiny sink and returned them to their drawer. She put the crackers away and gave the table a swipe with a none-too-clean towel, then sat down across from him.

She said, "You're darn tootin' you don't know anything about modern art, hombre. I can see you don't get the scenario. Here's how it works. They don't pay you anything to be an artist anymore. They've got just about every other category of work there is, in the Production Congress. Even education is a guild. But not the arts. Take writing. Some funker writes a book and submits it to the National Data Banks. They list it a half dozen ways from Tuesday; fiction, nonfiction, poetry, or whatever. They list it by category; novel, novelette, short story, essay, or whatever. They list it by subject; a suspense story, science fiction, love romance, travel, or whatever. They list it by the author's name. And they have on tap every review written about it. There it is, in the data banks. If anybody wants to read it, they can dial it and get it on their library-booster screen."

Ted Swain said sourly, "Yeah, wizard. I've often wondered what the writer gets out of it. Why he bothers."

"Don't be a flat. He gets what any artist got, down through the ages, since the Cro-Magnons did their paintings on the walls of the caves and the tribal story-teller recited the tribal traditions and lays to those who gathered around the fire to hear him. The artist gets the acclaim of his fellow man—if he deserves it. In the past, the poor funker had to toady to others— editors, publishers and eventually readers—in order to make an income. Now he writes what he damn well pleases. He gets his Universal Guaranteed Income, just as much as does anyone else, and he kisses nobody's, but nobody's, ass. Why, back in the Middle Ages an artist of any type, who wasn't wealthy himself, had to get a wealthy patron to support him; Leonardo and Michelangelo, among artists, Machiavelli and Dante among other writers. Can you imagine what that meant, licking the boots of those half-assed aristocrats, so you could eat?"

"Well, I more or less understand the writer in present society, but how about the painter?"

"Much the same thing. I think it started in France, back in the 1960s or so. Some bright-eyed type came up with a new system of duplicating paintings. The thing was, though, you couldn't paint on canvas or paper, or whatever. You had to paint on Presdwood-duplicator board and you had to paint with quick-drying, metallic acrylic paint.

"All right. Today, an artist does his thing and submits it to the National Data Banks. Like a writer's work, it is listed and crosslisted. Name of the painter, school of painting, type of painting, portrait, landscape, abstract, or whatever. They even list it by the size of the painting. And they list whatever comments the painting receives from the critics. All right. If anybody is interested they take a look at it on their library-booster screen. If the interest continues, they buy a copy. It costs practically nothing. Just the expense of turning out one more copy."

She went over to her autobar and dialed two more drinks, then brought them back. They were in cordial glasses.

Ted said, "I've already had four drinks today and it's only a little past noon."

"This is Khalua, from Mexico. One of the top half

69

dozen liqueurs in the world. Drink up; you'll need it when I get you into bed."

He took it and sipped. It was obviously based on coffee and was delicious. He had never heard of it before.

He said, "Yes, that's all very fine. But how about the original? The only paintings I have in my house I inherited from my parents. They're all originals. Don't some people prefer to have the original, rather than a reproduction?"

"What original?" she said. "These so-called reproductions are identical to the painting the artist made. Not even he can tell the difference. I mean, they *really* reproduce them."

"Oh," he said. "As I told you, I'm a specialist in ethnology. American Indians; ultimate subspecialization, the Aztecs at the time of the Spanish Conquest. Possibly, some day, the way things are going, I'll have to add a subspecialization to that. But as it stands now, I know everything about the Aztecs that there is to know. I wish I could spend some time down there, discovering some new data. At any rate, that's my field. I'm at sea when it comes to your field."

She said, "You ought to come along with us."

"How do you mean?"

"Didn't Bat Hardin tell you? We're treking all the way down through Latin America. One of the big reasons is that a large percentage of our artists want to paint, sculpt or write about the Indian civilizations. The Aztecs, the Mayans, further down, the Incas, in Peru. If you came along you'd be a wealth of background. You'd be able to tell us what to look for, explain what we see, that sort of razzle."

"You know, you tempt me," he said. "However, I've finally gotten my big chance. I'll be able to get my degree and teach, or hold down some other job in the field. Your friend, Bat, makes a pretty good argument for an artist not working in the world as it is, but it doesn't apply to me. I want to do my share."

70

"Let's get this show on the road," she said. "I want to get back to my painting."

She led the way back into the bedroom, at the far end of her mobile home. It was surprisingly large considering that it was in a trailer. Large, with a double bed and a connecting bath that had a tub as well as a shower. It would seem that the clutter of the front room was not allowed in the bedroom. The decor was feminine and neat.

She turned and faced him, a slight smile on her face as she automated the zip at the side of her shorts and let them fall away. She had a surprisingly large thatch of fine golden pubic hair.

She said, "Well, like me?"

"Yes." His voice was slightly hoarse.

She stepped closer to him and looked full into his eyes as she fumbled with his kilts. "How do you get these damn things off?"

Together they undressed him. She sat back on the bed and for a moment he stood there, looking down at her. She said, "Zoroaster, what a wizard of a tool. How long's it been hard like that?"

"Practically since I first met you."

"What a way to go through a meal," she said sardonically. She looked up into his face, her eyes sleepy and sensual. "Want me to kiss it?"

"Of course," he said. His voice was really hoarse now.

"Then step closer."

He stepped closer and closed his eyes in an agony of pleasure. "For me, this is best when it's mutual."

"All right," she said, falling back on the bed and making room for him to stretch out beside her, head to feet.

Later on, when sex had become meaningless, they laid on their backs, staring up at the ceiling.

Sue Benny said, "Like a pot cigarette?"

"Do you have any hashish fudge or marmalade?"

"No, just cigarettes."

"No, thanks."

71

"I should have had one before you started to poke me. I like to be a bit high when I get poked."

He said, out of a clear sky, "Have you ever read any of the older novels? Those set back in the middle of the last century, or, even more so, before the First World War?"

"Sure. *Gone With the Wind*, and all. I was a great reader when I was a kid. Especially romances."

He said musingly, "Remember how they dealt with sex, with the relationships between men and women in general?"

Her laugh was more like a giggle. "Yeah, it was a real razzle. Sometimes the sexiest they'd get would be for the hombre to kiss her once in the last chapter."

"As an anthropologist, I sometimes wonder how the big change came about. How, and when, for that matter."

"No big question about that," she said. "And for that matter I wonder just how big the change really was. I sometimes suspect that there was always just about as much poking going on then as there is now. They simply hid it."

He shook his head. "No. No, there wasn't. For one thing, it was harder for young people to get together, even if that's what they had in mind. I suppose the coming of the automobile was the first big breakthrough. It allowed the kids to drive out and get into each other's pants."

"I would have said the coming of the early pills and other birth-control devices that really worked. All of a sudden a girl didn't have to worry about being knocked up and a boy didn't have to be worried about having to marry the girl he'd gotten an occasional piece of ass from."

"How about Women's Lib?"

"That too. From then on in, there was less and less of the Victorian-period crud about women being the weaker and more modest sex." She laughed again. "They really began poking in earnest."

He said, "Then the reversal of censorship. The

72

legalization of what they used to call 'pornography.' All of a sudden the kids could find out exactly what it was all about, and obviously wanted to try it immediately."

She stirred her body luxuriously. "Imagine what it was like in the old days to be physically able to poke when you were about thirteen and then not getting an opportunity to do it, at least to any extent, until you were in your early twenties. Ten damn years shot to hell! I'm surprised they weren't all driven drivel-happy."

Sue Benny looked over at her bedmate. "For Christ's sake, are you one of these hombres who gets a stiffy just talking about it?"

"Mind?"

"No. Got any more fancy ideas? To hell with my painting."

An hour later, they were really satiated.

Sue Benny said, "Look, what were you going to be doing for the rest of the day, Paul Bunyan?"

"Bunyan? The name's Ted Swain."

"You haven't done as much reading as you put up to have. Paul Bunyan was a legendary lumberjack. He could do anything, twenty times over what any other man could."

Ted pretended to groan. "Twenty times! Don't you ever tire, woman?"

"Seldom. That's why I like you. You pull half a dozen orgasms out of a mopsy while you're having one. I haven't come so much in my life. What did you plan to do for the rest of the day?"

"I thought I'd be able to check out at least one more commune."

"Too late. Why don't you stay here for the night, and find out more about this one? We could eat over at the autocafeteria. They've got a wizard of a one on this site."

He sighed. "You just talked me into it."

Chapter Nine

Ted Swain had forgotten to dismiss his electrosteamer the night before. Not that it was important. The rental on cars was low, and his credit account was healthy, usually healthy; as a full-time scholar he had few extravagances. Nevertheless, as a rule he made a point of returning a vehicle when he wasn't actually using it. It kept down vehicle congestion. It was one of the big breakthroughs that the new society had inaugurated. In the old days, when most cars were privately owned, the majority of them spent at least three quarters of their time parked in garages or on the steets. Each family had one, two, or even three. The country had been ass-deep in cars. Now, when you had need, you summoned one; a two-seater, if there was but one or two of you wanting transportation, a sedan if there were three to six, a minibus for groups, or an even larger vehicle, if required. And when you were through with it, you dismissed it to return automatically to the nearest autopark and garage. Whatever you summoned, it was always in top repair.

He was about to climb into his electrosteamer, his mind still dwelling on the pleasures of Sue Benny, when Mike Latimer drove up and parked beside him.

The news commentator seemed equally surprised to see Ted Swain. He said, "What in the name of holy

Zoroaster are you doing here, this early in the morning?"

Ted said, "The early bird catches the worm."

"Wizard, but who likes worms?"

Ted came over and leaned on the side of Latimer's vehicle. "I've started my probe into the communes. This is one of the first."

Mike said, "Actually, I came around to see if I could pick up an item for the broadcast. You know, Mobile Art Colony Shaping Up For South American Safari. You've obviously spent the night. What do you think of the layout?"

Ted Swain considered the question. "Well, for one thing, do you realize that not a single person in this commune works? At least, not in regular industry. They're all either on Universal Guaranteed Income, or are sponging on others who are. And now they're removing themselves from the country. Even if one was called up at the next muster, he'd simply drop out and live off the community."

Mike Latimer thought about it. "As far back as the 1960s, Richard Bellman of the Rand Corporation upped with the belief that two percent of the working force would be able to produce all that the country could consume by the year 2000. And now, here we are. We don't need these dropouts. If they want to take off for South America, why, let 'em go."

"It's nearer to ten percent, isn't it?"

"Something like that. But the majority of people employed today are in make-work jobs. Not really necessary. Something like featherbedding in the old days." He thought about it some more. "I sometimes wonder why people like myself bother to compete for a job. If the computers select you on muster day, you don't get much more pay than those unemployed."

"You're not reading the script," Ted Swain said. "It's a compulsion. Here I am in my thirties. Since childhood I've been goosed along the path of my latent abilities. My biggest interest in life is ethnology. I want to participate in the field so badly I can taste it. I *want* a job. I'm frustrated because I can't get one. The same must apply to you, but you've found fulfillment. You've got a job in the field you love."

"Yeah, I suppose so," Mike Latimer admitted. "Look, I've been thinking about this dissertation of yours and came up with a few more communes in this area. Have you heard about New Athens?"

"Don't believe so."

"Not far away. Over near Lake Hill. They're all athletes. Interested in practically nothing but body building and sports. Come to think of it, I ought to run over there and check them out. Make an interesting item. Then there's Jissom."

"Jissom?" Ted Swain snorted. "Why don't they just call the place 'cum'?"

Mike ignored him. "It's a youth commune, located near Bearsville. Nobody over thirty. Rumor is that they're drug-culture types. Not only pot, but evidently from time to time they send one of their number down to Mexico to get in a supply of sacred mushrooms. Somebody told me they were trying to make contact with Peru to get coca leaves. What kind of a razzle is chewing coca?"

Ted drew on his knowledge as an anthropologist. "Goes back to Inca times. Cocaine is derived from coca. Actually, though, coca isn't addictive. It's a stimulant, but not really a narcotic. Jissom, eh? I suppose I ought to put it on my list. Well, I guess I'll shove off. Look up the town cop, Bat Hardin. Nice guy. Stay away from Sue Benny Voss. She's my girl."

Mike Latimer shook his head. "I don't know how you do it. You're as ugly as a pig, and you get more ass than anybody I know."

Ted said, with considerable dignity, "I resemble that remark."

Mike began climbing out of his car as Ted got into his. "See you later," Latimer said. "Sue Benny, eh? Sue Benny. If she'll put out for you, she'll put out for anybody."

On his way back to his home in West Hurley, Ted Swain continued to mull over his situation. In actuality, he was surprised that Englebrecht had come up with the assignment. It was not to the advantage of the old boy to see created too many new academicians in his own field, since only from their ranks could he be bounced, if he were bounced. Ted had suspected for years that the other had been actually blocking his achievement of the degree. But now this.

Getting bounced from your position applied particularly in those fields where human knowledge was developing most rapidly. As far back as the middle of the 1950s, the physicist Robert Oppenheimer had pointed out that human knowledge was doubling every eight years. This in turn meant that the education with which you emerged from had a half-life of four years. That is, in four years half of everything you had learned was antiquated, and you were obviously on the scrap heap unless you returned to the university and took refresher courses, or, as an alternative, studied for a few hours each day at home.

The physical sciences were the worst. You had to run as desperately as Alice in Looking-Glass country, just to keep up with where you were. But the social sciences were different and it was there that Englebrecht had his edge. Social sciences didn't evolve in such a geometric progression. Evolve, yes, but at not such a breakneck speed. In archaeology, for instance, some great breakthroughs might come, such as carbon dating, and later even more accurate dating processes, and revolutionize knowledge of past cultures, but largely it was a more plodding affair. And certainly when you achieved the rarified heights of the field held by Franz Englebrecht, your experience and entrenched position in your genre went far toward negating the A.Q.'s of the youngsters coming up.

Ted Swain felt a certain bitterness about the nature of things in his chosen field. As a director of dissertations, Englebrecht received equal credit with any of the candidates he supposedly tutored, both on scientific papers or on the dissertation for a doctor's or academician's degree. And since he was department head, he was director of all higher degrees in anthropology and ethnology. There was no possible manner in which to take your degree without him robbing you of half of the honor.

What real ability did Franz Englebrecht have to hold down such a position? Ted Swain sometimes wondered.

He had read of the system of breaking down the types of occupations into primary, secondary, tertiary and quaternary. Primary jobs were fishing, hunting, forestry, agriculture and mining. Secondary occupations were concerned with processing the products of a primary occupation. Tertiary dealt with rendering services to primary and secondary occupations, teachers, for instance, or police and firemen. And quaternary occupations were those that rendered services to tertiary occupations or to each other. They were the top jobs, the agencies of government, the professions, the top managers of production, that sort of thing.

With primary jobs it was easy enough for the computers to come up with the Ability Quotients of the potential employees in the field. Easy enough to measure a man's ability in mining, agriculture, or whatever. And the same applied to the secondary. Easy enough to determine a man's efficiency in working in a steel mill, an auto factory, or whatever. Tertiary? It became a bit more difficult. Judging a teacher, an artist, a policeman, even, is another thing. But above all, the quaternary occupations were nearly exempt from the judgment of computers. Not quite, but almost. The quaternary occupations took in one another's wash, so to speak, and since experience, rather than Ability Quotient, was so all-important, your position depended sweepingly upon the opinions of your colleagues. Ted suspected that there was a good deal of you-scratch-my-back-and-I'll-scratch-yours involved.

Back at the house, he dismissed his electrosteamer and entered. There were no messages on his TV phone.

He went back into his study, took a stimmy pill, seated himself at the desk and activated the National Data Bank library booster.

He needed more background, damn it. He didn't even know what questions to ask of these people. In these days of specilization, if you were going to get anywhere in whatever field it was you worked, you for all practical purposes cut yourself free of any other involvement. He knew one hell of a lot about primitive social systems, primitive communes, if you would, but he was blank on modern ones.

All right. He had checked out, the day before, More's *Utopia* and Plato's *Republic*. But surely there had been something between those days and the present. He began researching the National Data Banks again.

And yes, he came upon one that had existed comparatively recently. In the 1920s, to be exact. Llano, a cooperative in Louisiana consisting of more than a thousand persons at its peak. Evidently, a group of like-minded communards ... no, he didn't think he liked that term. Should he call them 'communitarians'? At any rate, the Llano people had amalgamated their resources and bought up a lumber town which had been abandoned when the supply of trees ran out. They had initiated it in the early 1920s and it had continued for at least a couple of decades before folding.

Yes, he could use Llano as an example of an early commune. What else?

He found the Father Divine movement, begun during the Depression years of the 1930s. Very similar, in many respects, to the modern commune, if he had any idea at all of the latter, and, in actuality, he had already admitted that he didn't. Supposedly a religious leader—his followers hailed him as God—in actuality Father Divine's organization was economic. A hundred or more of them would pool resources and buy up an old mansion, usually in Upstate New York. Some would be unemployed carpenters, some electricians, some plumbers, some farmers, some cooks, and so on.

They all pitched in. The mansions were refurbished, extensive gardens were cultivated, the women made quilts for the beds, the men made furniture, the mechanics bought stone-age jalopies and rebuilt them. All worked. Those who could got jobs on the outside and all income went into the community kitty.

Ted grunted. It would seem that it had gone surprisingly well until the Depression ended and members of the Father Divine "heavens" got jobs in the shipyards at a $100 or more a week.

A thought occurred to him. In that first chapter could he ring in the early Christians as described in the Acts of the Apostles? Why not? They lived in what amounted to communes. And how about the Essenes as described in the Dead Sea Scrolls? They lived in a commune, didn't they?

He was beginning to warm to his work when the desk TV phone buzzed. He deactivated the library booster and switched on the phone screen. It was Academician Englebrecht, his facial expression as insipid as always.

"Swain, my boy," he said fondly, as though Ted was indeed his highly beloved son.

Inwardly Ted Swain winced, but he said, "Good morning, sir."

"Already embarked on the project?" his director asked heartily.

"Well, yes, sir. This morning I've been researching material for preliminary chapters, origins of the commune. Plato's *Republic*, the Essenes, the early Christians of the time of the Acts . . ."

A scowl came to the other's face and he interrupted. "See here, Swain. At this stage I think it more important that you begin checking up on current communes, personally. You can do your research later, in the National Data Banks data. At any rate, can you come over here immediately? There's someone I want you to meet."

"Why . . . yes, sir. Certainly."

When the other's face had faded from the screen,

Ted continued to look at it ruefully. It would seem that once you actually got working on your dissertation, old man Englebrecht rode tight herd on you. He wondered why in the hell Englebrecht was so keen to get him out into the field, rather than allow him to spend some preliminary time finding out just what it was he was supposedly looking for. How was he going to be able to compare present-day communes to those of the past if he didn't know what those of the past were like? He was up on primitive communes, but not on those between prehistory and the present.

He shrugged it off and came to his feet. Franz Englebrecht was the boss. Ted Swain could put up with just about anything if it finally led to his degree and a job.

He retraced his route of two days before, winding up in the entranceway of apartment 355, as before. Brian Fitz was there, impatiently fingering his silky Van Dyke, his red lips in a pettish moue.

He said, "Good heavens, Doctor Swain, the academician is awaiting you."

Ted looked at him. "Take it up with the Transportation Guild. I came as quickly as they'd bring me."

Fitz, miffed, turned and with a swish led the way to the escape sanctum. He was a queerie, all right, Ted Swain decided.

Englebrecht was at the desk again, his pink, well-larded face beaming welcome. Next to the desk, seated in a leather comfort chair, was a stranger. No, not exactly a stranger. Ted Swain had seen him on various occasions on TV broadcasts.

"Swain, my boy," Englebrecht burbled. "I want you to meet an old classmate and dear friend, Henry Neville. Hank, this is the young chap I was telling you about, Doctor Theodore Swain. Quite an authority on primitive communes and now researching present-day ones, to compare them."

Henry Clark Neville was director of the region's National Security Forces, which was, in short, a combination of the local, state and national police of the previous society. The NSF handled everything from traffic cops to the tasks once held down by the FBI, the Secret Service, and even some of the duties of the CIA. Neville was a smaller man than Ted Swain would have expected from having seen him on the screen, possibly five and a half feet tall, thin and waspish of face, thin of lips and with a graying mustache. It was a ferretlike face. He didn't look like the type to attract many friends, but evidently old man Englebrecht was one of them.

The police official came to his feet and shook hands with a bony, very dry hand. He snapped a nod and said, "It's about time they were investigated, Doctor."

Brian Fitz had brought up another chair.

When all were seated, save Fitz, who hovered in the background, Ted said, "How is that, sir?" to Neville.

"By this time they number literally millions of malcontents and even outright criminals, and for all practical purposes we have no records of them."

Ted Swain was surprised. "Well, why not? I would think that your officers would have no difficulty entering any commune and finding out whatever you wished."

Neville shook his head in irritation. "They clam up. They'll often give misinformation, deliberately. Some of them have actually destroyed their transceivers, which is illegal in itself. It prevents the government from getting in immediate touch with a person, if required. They hide their fugitives, move from one commune to another, or often they move their whole shebang, if it's one of the new mobile towns, without notifying anyone at all. It's practically impossible to keep tabs on many of them."

"Destroy their transceivers? Fugitives? But ... you can't live in this society without a transceiver, issued by the government to every citizen. It's your portable phone, it's your identification, it's your contact with the data banks, it's your voting booth. You can't buy anything without it. You can't collect your Universal

Guaranteed Income. You can't rent a car. You can't do anything," Ted said.

Neville said grimly, "You can if you live in a commune. They take care of each other. Those that retain their transceivers and collect their UGI buy supplies for the others. Many of them live on a fraction of what a normal person expects." He snorted contemptuously. "Yes, fugitives. Suppose, for instance, that you are selected on job-muster day for a job you don't wish to take. By law, you are obligated to take it or lose your citizenship rights and your Universal Guaranteed Income. They couldn't care less. They join a commune and the others support them. Lazy funkers! Or suppose a man is an actual criminal, a rapist, or whatever. He can disappear into the commune culture and we really have our work cut out finding him."

In actuality, what Neville was saying wasn't as new as all that to Ted Swain. Bat Hardin had mentioned that the mobile art colony operated as a community, pooling its resources and if any of its members lost their rights to UGI, for whatever reason, they were taken care of out of the New Woodstock combined fund.

Englebrecht was saying smoothly, "Of course, of course. And I have no doubt, Hank, that Doctor Swain's investigations will be of considerable interest to you."

Ted said unhappily, "I didn't think in terms of whatever information I obtained being used for anything other than my dissertation."

The NSF director looked at him sharply and rapped, "What is your opinion of our present socioeconomic system, Doctor Swain?"

Ted was set back. "Why, I'm in favor of it, obviously. For the first time in history man is truly free. Each has equal opportunity, and there is an abundance for all. Who can argue against utopia?"

"Sage!" Neville said approvingly. "But there can be cancers even in utopia, and we must cut them out. As a patriotic American, Doctor, I expect you to keep your

83

eyes open and report to my offices any divergencies against our institutions. These communes are potential hotbeds of subversion."

Subversion? Ted Swain could only think of his own West Hurley. Or, for that matter, of Lesbos and New Woodstock. He hadn't had an inkling of subversion. As a matter of fact, he couldn't remember ever having met a subversive in his life.

Englebrecht beamed. "Of course, Swain will cooperate, Hank." He puffed out his cheeks and added in heavy-handed humor, "If he doesn't, it will be a snowy summer before he ever earns that academician's degree."

Ted Swain said, still displeased with the whole thing, "If I run into anything of an illegal subversive nature, I'll certainly pass it on to you, Mr. Neville. But, frankly, I haven't been expecting such matters to crop up. From what I understand, most, if not all, of these communes are based on some theme such as art, sports, nudism, back-to-nature movements, that sort of thing."

"Don't let them fool you," Neville said, the wasp in his voice. "On the surface, yes. But underneath there is ferment. In particular I'd like you to keep your ears open for anything political. If you dig something out, get names, Doctor."

"Political?"

"Definitely We pride ourselves, we Americans, on our two-party system, the Democratic Republicans and the Progressive Americans. But there's nothing to prevent a new party from emerging. Nothing as yet, at least. However, do you realize that less than ten percent of our population are really useful members of society? Ninety percent are drones and as things are now that ninety percent could swing the vote and put over any changes they wanted."

Ted Swain was tempted to ask what changes those might be, but he was building up a feeling of unreality about all this. Henry Neville, as director of this region's National Security Forces, obviously was obligated to keep an eye on any potential subversives, but surely he was seeing bugaboos where none existed.

The academician said, "And now, my boy, when do you plan to get out and start your investigation into these communes?"

"I've already started, sir. Yesterday I dropped in on Lesbos and New Woodstock. I drew a blank at the first. The theme there was lesbianism and men aren't welcome. I had better luck at the mobile art colony."

"I'll expect a complete report. Let me have in detail all that you learned."

Ted Swain looked at him. "A report?"

"Of course, of course. I want a report on every commune you investigate. By perusing them I'll undoubtedly be able to give you pointers, suggestions toward making your dissertation acceptable."

Chapter Ten

After he had left the tower-
ing hi-rise which housed his director of dissertation,
Ted Swain thought it over. Well, one thing, if both
George Dollar of the National Data Banks and Henry
Neville of the National Security Forces were both hot
about this project of his, it would seem that he could
hardly fail to secure his degree, assuming that he was
able to put over the research acceptably. They threw
one hell of a lot of clout in this vicinity and were
seemingly among Englebrecht's closest friends.

He sat in his electrosteamer and looked at the list
that he had so far accumulated of communes in the
vicinity. He supposed that later on he'd have to make
trips of more distance but as of now there were enough
at close range to keep him busy.

New Athens, near Lake Hill. Who had given him
that? Mike Latimer, probably. Gloria, over at Lesbos,
had mentioned New Tangier and Gomorrah but both
of them had off-beat sexual themes. New Athens was
supposed to be a commune of athletes.

Well, New Athens it was. He brought the car's area
map from the glove compartment and looked up the
coordinates of Lake Hill, then dialed them.

As the vehicle sped along the underground expressway, he inwardly recapitulated the scene in

Englebrecht's escape sanctum. A thorough report on each commune he visited was wanted, with an ear for any hint of subversion or interest in things political. Why members of communes didn't have as much right to be as political as anyone else, he didn't understand. But the hell with it. He was going to make a success of this dissertation if it was the second to the last thing he ever did. Dying being the last.

He emerged at Lake Hill, a small village in the old Catskill tradition, and asked directions of the first pedestrian and then, as instructed, headed up into the foothills of Overlook Mountain. It was superlative countryside, particularly at this time of year, early fall. The red of the maples, the yellow of the oaks, the browns of the elms. The Catskills hadn't been as polluted, corrupted and destroyed as so much of America had during the 20th Century. It had been a comparatively easy task to clean it up, to restore it to the beauty it had boasted in the early part of the century. There was an occasional meadow, an occasional apple orchard. It was all but a national park. From time to time he would pass an old-fashioned farm house, wood smoke issuing from the chimney. His faint smile held an element of ironic envy. Weirds. He knew of the type. Those who completely rejected the modern home in suburbia, pseudocity or even commune, and lived in the past. It had its points, he was sure, but still ninety-five percent of the population considered them "weirds."

The narrow way actually became dirt. It had been a long time since he had driven on a dirt road. It emphasized how much the area resembled the New England of yesteryear.

His first glimpse of New Athens set him back.

He came upon an athletic field so large that two football contests could have been going on at once, with room left over for a baseball game.

He came to a halt and stared.

Neither football nor baseball were in process, but damned near every other sport he had ever heard of was. Perhaps a thousand men, women and childen were doing everything from throwing javelins and discuses, to racing, to jumping (both broad and high), to pole vaulting, to weight lifting, to boxing, to wrestling, to everything else. The thought came to Ted's mind, *a poor man's Olympics*. Most seemed to be working out on their own, except the boxers and wrestlers. There was nothing involving teams.

It was their get-up that had him staring. Some of the men were completely nude, though most wore short white kilts, hemmed in color, and sandals. Most of the women wore light short-skirted playsuits, though some, like the men, were topless. All very Grecian in appearance.

They all, men, women and kids seemed to be working up a sweat with boundless enthusiasm. It wearied Ted Swain simply to watch.

Beyond the sports field small brick houses stretched in every direction. Possibly half a mile away a long building, two stories high, gave hint of an administrative center. Ted headed for it. He was on manual controls and as he drove he took in the athletic field from the sides of his eyes. Zoroaster! He passed two muscle-bound types armed with wooden swords and shields and with football helmets on their heads. They were whaling away at each other with more elan than skill. Ted Swain shook his head.

As he got closer to his goal, it came to him why he was frowning—vague recognition. The building was a reproduction of the Stoa of Attalos. The original, in Athens, Greece, was a two-storied structure with 21 shops opening off of a deep-colonnaded porch. It had been reconstructed by the Rockefeller Foundation, a duplication of the market built by Attalos, King of Pergamum. In ancient times, the stoas had been utilized by such philosophers as Socrates for much of their teaching.

The streets now were cobblestoned. Another bit of razzle to reproduce the Golden Age, he supposed.

These people took their communal theme seriously. He shook his head again. Everything but chariots.

Most of the pedestrians he passed were also in pseudo-Grecian costume, though not all. Those who were in modern dress looked incongruous, in comparison. The setting called for the ancient garb.

He realized now that the small houses were another attempt to reproduce the times of Pericles. The Greeks had never bothered to fancy up their homes. Not for them the mansions that were to prevail under the Romans. For them a house was a place in which to eat, sleep, and to pen up wife and children. A man spent his time in the public buildings, the stoas, the taverns, the baths, the libraries, the marketplace.

Ted Swain pulled up before the main entrance of the stoa and sat there for a moment before alighting. The passersby didn't pay any attention to him. He sighed and got out, after first checking his microphone bug. It seemed to be operational. He flicked the tiny stud to activate it, then headed for the door.

In the interior, it became obvious that the New Athenians weren't going to be held to exterior manifestations of duplicating of the Greek civilization of old. The hall contained a score of marble statues of gods and goddesses, of Hercules complete with lion's skin and club, of Achilles, or some other Iliad hero, in full armor. There were stone benches and wooden chairs of ancient design, undoubtedly copied from the Greek rooms of some museum.

Ted Swain approached a middle-aged type swathed in what would seem to be a bedsheet, in contrast to the younger people going by in white kilts and sandals, or in draped ankle-length gowns.

He said, "I'm a newcomer, looking for information about New Athens. Could you tell me whom I should see?"

The other took him in and said, "You'd profit by living in New Athens, young man. You're much too flabby, although you need more meat on your bones."

89

"All right," Ted admitted. "So whom do I see to find out more about your commune?"

The critic of his physique directed him.

Ted Swain went down the hall to the door indicated. It was open so he walked in without knocking. There was no identity screen, presumably because they hadn't had them in the Golden Age.

There were three desks, two of them occupied. That in the center, the largest, had behind it an older man than Ted Swain had thus far seen in New Athens. He too was draped in the toga-type gown which Ted insisted upon thinking of as a bedsheet. His hair was a smooth white at the temples, blending into iron-gray on top. He had an economical smile, emotionless gray eyes and a soft unhurried voice.

He said, "What can I do for you?"

Ted said, "I'm Theodore Swain . . ."

"Aristotle Burton," the other said, nodding.

Ted went on. "I've heard about New Athens and thought I'd drop by to find out more about it." He was playing it about halfway between Lesbos and New Woodstock. He hadn't said he was interested in joining up, but on the other hand he hadn't come out into the open as he had with Bat Hardin.

The other nodded again and said easily, "That is why we are here. Terpsichore, my dear."

The occupant of the other desk was a girl in the usual white, flowing dress. Her eyes took Ted in. They were lovely eyes, wide-spaced and a cool blue-green, beneath a bold sweep of dark brows. She came to her feet gracefully. Gracefully indeed. Only the Indian sari showed off femininity as well as her draped dress did.

"I'll be glad to show you around," she said.

Ted, preparing to follow her, said to Aristotle Burton, "Thank you," and received another nod in response. He couldn't quite believe that name. Nor Terpsichore, either. Wasn't that the Greek goddess of the dance? He assumed that they took Greek names upon joining the commune.

In the corridor beyond, Terpsichore said, "There is a

taverna across the street, if you would like to have a glass of retsina while we talk." Her voice was throaty, sexy.

"What's a taverna, although I suppose I can guess, but what's retsina? I thought that in my time I'd drunk everything not thick enough to eat."

"A bar, and wine," she said with a quirk of her full lips.

"I'd think athletic types such as yourselves would be teetotalers. Not that I'm complaining."

She led the way—her walk was a dream of grace—from the stoa across the cobblestoned street, saying, "The Greeks probably invented wine. It is usually accredited to Dionysus, the god of the vine. It is undoubtedly the most healthful of alcoholic beverages. We drink it in moderation."

They entered a simple, single-room building with a sign hanging before the door depicting a bunch of red grapes, but without wording. There were some twenty tables inside, and a bar without stools. The place was mostly unoccupied. To Ted Swain's surprise, there was a bartender. He hadn't seen a live bartender since he'd been a youth. Ultramation had dispensed with them.

Even as they found seats, Terpsichore surmised his reaction and said, "We avoid automation to the point possible. We who are unemployed take turns at such tasks as being bartenders, waiters, town criers and so forth."

Seemingly, there was but a limited wine list. The bartender came over with two bottles and two wine glasses and put them down on the table. He tipped a wink to the girl and returned to the bar.

"I recommend the white retsina," Terpsichore said.

There were both white and red. Ted Swain took up the white and poured for them. Although white, the wine was unchilled. He assumed that the ancient Greeks didn't utilize ice.

They held their glasses up to each other and she said, "Cheers, cheers."

91

Ted said, "There is no God but Allah," and they drank.

His eyes bugged, he almost sputtered the greater part of the drink out. He stared down into the glass reproachfully.

"What in the name of holy Zoroaster is that?"

She tinkled a laugh. "I warned you. It's retsina. That piney taste is resin, which is added to the wine after fermentation. You see, the Greeks lined their wineskins with resin to help preservation. They got used to the flavor, something like the Scots got used to the taste of peat in their scotch and, after peat was no longer used in the distillation, added the flavor artificially. The Greeks down through the ages have added the resin flavor to their wine."

"And anything the ancient Greeks did is wizard with you people, eh?"

She was looking at him oddly, a faint frown forming above her eyes. "But, of course. Surely you knew that was the basis of our commune. The Greeks realized the highest culture the world has ever seen. We attempt to revive it."

"I thought we Americans were realizing the highest culture the world has ever seen," Ted said, taking another cautious sip of the wine. Could you actually develop a taste for this?

"Possibly it potentially could be," she said.

"I thought the Greek economy was based on slavery. It was all very good for the male Athenian citizen, for instance, but each citizen averaged eight slaves. Just how much of that high culture was appreciated by those slaves?"

"That's true," she smiled. "Only the male citizens enjoyed the Golden Age. But today we are all citizens. We have slaves . . ."

"You have *slaves*?" he blurted.

". . . but today our slaves are machines. Ultramation, computerized industry, has taken over practically all labor. Less than ten percent of the residents of New Athens are involved in national industry."

"All of them work in this vicinity?"

"Yes, of course."

"Suppose on job-muster day one of your commune gets a position that takes him to, say, Region Four, the Southwest. Then he has to give up living here." He hesitated and added, "Or do you do what some of the other communes practice? That is, let him give up his Universal Guaranteed Income and the rest of you support him out of the community fund?"

She looked at him and her expression was one of mild surprise. "Why, no. He would most likely transfer to the nearest deme in that area."

"Deme?"

"That's what we call our communes. Let me see, in the Southwest there are New Sparta, New Delos, New Thebes . . ."

"Wait a minute. You mean to tell me these Greek revival communes are spread all over the country?"

"Why, yes. Didn't you know that? I imagine there's some half a million of us in all."

"Half a million?" He was flabbergasted. Something came to him. "How are you politically? I mean, do you vote in a block?"

He watched another frown put a small uneven line in the clear skin above her eyes. "No. Largely we abstain from politics. I suppose you could say that so far as we of the Greek revival are concerned, Robert Owen lives."

"Robert Owen? What has he to do with it?"

"Why, he was more or less the father of the modern commune. He scorned politics, thinking them a sham, a means of hoodwinking the people into the false belief that they were free and in control of their government."

Ted Swain shook his head. "I've gone through life without hearing Owen's name more than once or twice. This past several days, looking into the communes, I've heard it several times."

She shrugged slightly, a motion that jiggled her perfect breasts. He couldn't help noticing that the material of her gown was so diaphanous that the pinkness of her nipples could faintly be detected.

She said, "I suppose that most residents of communes are conscious of Robert Owen. But now you'll wish to see the town a bit. Shall we go?" She came to her feet, a derisive half-smile smoothing her full lips. "Particularly since you don't seem to appreciate retsina."

He grinned ruefully as he stood, too. "An acquired taste, undoubtedly, but I'm wondering how in the hell you stick to the stuff long enough to acquire it. How do I pay for this bottle, by the way?"

She led the way to the door. "You don't. We have our own vineyards and work them cooperatively, those of us who don't hold down jobs. The wine is on New Athens."

They strolled down the cobblestoned street. There were no vehicles and he commented on the fact.

"We hate them," she said. "Obviously, we can't do without, entirely. Some of us have to go to work and so forth. But we keep them out of sight in a car park on the outskirts of town."

Everywhere were the signs of the town's theme; tennis courts, swimming pools, jai alai courts, an archery range. In the distance he could see a golf course.

"A golf course?" he said. "I thought that was a Scotch game."

"We're not fanatical. You mentioned looking into the communes. Then your interest isn't particularly just New Athens?"

He had to tread carefully now. He said, "No, not just New Athens. Up until a couple of days ago, I'd hardly more than heard of communes. But they're becoming increasingly fascinating. Over at New Woodstock, the mobile art colony, they suggested I come along on their projected trip to South America."

They came upon a beautifully done park. In its dead center was a duplication of the Theseum, the best-preserved of all Greek temples.

"Oh, *come on* now," Ted Swain protested. "Don't

94

tell me you people practice the ancient Greek religion. Zoroaster! That's carrying it too far."

She laughed her tinkle of a laugh. "Not Zoroaster, but Zeus. But no, not really. We pay lip service to mythology but none of us, so far as I know, at least, truly believe in the Olympian gods. Are you religious?"

"Well, not really. My parents used to be Methodists, or Presbyterians, or something, but it was one of those going-to-church-once-a-year, at Easter or Christmas, deals. If you'd asked them if they believed in God, the answer would have been an indignant 'Of course,' but in actuality they weren't truly religious. I suppose I'm an agnostic."

She said, "I'm afraid that's the way we are about the Olympians but at least they're a bit more interesting than the Jewish Jehovah. It must have been a grim people who dreamed that god up. Now Apollo and Dionysus are another thing, not to speak of Cupid. At any rate, the temple is a pleasant, quiet place to go and meditate. But you've seen the town. Would you like to enter one of the houses and check the layout? Possibly we'll talk you into joining up after all."

"Wizard," he said.

"My own place is just over here." She led the way, looking at him with her blue-green eyes. "That is, if you have no objection to entering a bachelor girl's abode."

"This is the second time, in as many days, that I've pointed out that I'm queer for girls."

She made a moue and looked him up and down. "Indeed?"

"Yes, indeed."

She escorted him to one of the small brick houses. There was no identity screen on the door and she opened it manually.

The interior was Spartan by West Hurley standards. Comfortable enough, but Spartan. The living room, which the door opened directly into, didn't even have a TV screen on the wall. The furniture had obviously been copied from Greek sources; Ted assumed from

95

ancient paintings and the little that had come down through history to present-day museums. He suspected that some of it was Roman, rather than Greek. Pompeii had offered up quite a selection of early furniture though, admittedly, it had largely been Greek artisans who'd designed and executed Roman household needs.

He looked about him. "No kitchen?"

She said, "We eat in community dining halls. We avoid a good deal of ultramation, but there's just too much drudgery involved for each home in New Athens to prepare its own food, clean up and so forth."

"Sage," he said. "However, I'm an amateur chef."

"Once again, we're not fanatical about it. You could have a kitchen in your house, if you wanted." She turned and led the way again. "In here is the bedroom and bath."

He followed. The bedroom was as Spartan as the living room, but, at least, the bed looked ample.

She turned to face him, pulled the sash of her flowing gown. The gown fell away to her feet. Not only did Terpsichore wear no brassiere, but was equally innocent of other underclothing. Ted Swain felt his throat tense up. She was beautifully shaped, Aphrodite in pink marble. Her arms were limp at her sides.

"All right?" she said softly, her throat thick with sex.

He stepped closer, tipped up her chin with a forefinger. "With all these muscle boys in town, you pick a limp specimen like me?"

She cast her eyes down in mock demureness, and murmured, "I'm sure you're not always ... limp. You'd be surprised how much of their energy goes into that endless exercise. They don't have enough left to ... Here, let me help you with your clothes." She fumbled with his belt.

She stretched out on the bed, face down, and he sat on the edge and caressed her upper legs and her fabulous buttocks. He traced a finger down her spine and she sucked in breath.

He said, "I can't quite believe this. Is this part of the conducted tour Aristotle Burton told you to give me?"

She laughed softly. "Haven't you heard of the Greek hetaera?"

"Well, yes, but I didn't expect to encounter one." He was more than ready to take her.

Her legs were like satin; the palms of his hands slid smoothly over the backs of her thighs and calves. He saw the sparkle of fine blond hair in the sunlight that leaked through the venetian blinds, and felt the shape and tension of her slim muscles under his moving fingers. And he discovered that he could close his hand completely around her delicate ankles.

"Turn over," he said hoarsely.

"Why?" she murmured into her pillow. "Do me boy style. Haven't you heard about the Greeks?"

Chapter Eleven

Ted Swain was working on his reports to Englebrecht when Mike Latimer showed up the next day. Initially, he had played the disk upon which he had recorded all the conversations he'd had at the communes into the voco-typer and gotten it all on paper. He had reread it, snorting sour amusement at his razzle at Lesbos with the butch named Gloria, snorting more amusement at the sounds which issued forth on his occasions with first Sue Benny Voss and, the next day, with Terpsichore. The New Athens girl had let out a startled gasp at first entry; evidently he was larger than she had expected. Both times he had forgotten to turn off the bug.

The reports came hard. In actuality, he could think of precious little to put into them. Certainly nothing that would be of particular interest to Academician Englebrecht. He attempted to sort out and analyze the facts he had accumulated thus far, but the effort seemed only to lead him up blind alleys to stone walls.

Of course, he had thus far only investigated two of these mushrooming communes, but their investigation certainly gave him little that could go into a comparison of primitive and modern communes. Here this was, his big chance, and deep inside he felt that he was flubbing it. He simply didn't get the scenario.

There was a gentle buzz and he flicked the door identity screen switch on his TV phone. The face that faded in was that of Mike Latimer. He pushed the button to open the front door, then came to his feet and went into the living room to greet his visitor.

The other was dressed in Bermuda shorts, wore heavy walking shoes and carried a black thorn walking stick.

He waved the stick at Ted, in way of greeting, slumped down into a comfort chair and said, "Just passing by on a stroll and thought I'd drop in for a minute. How about a drink?"

"At this time of morning?" Ted growled, but motioned with his head at the autobar. "How about a glass of retsina?"

Mike struggled up from his chair and went over to the bar. "What's retsina?"

"Wine with resin in it."

"Sounds awful." Mike dialed himself a glass of ale.

"It is, but the Greeks used to drink it that way, so that's what they drink in New Athens. They do other things the Greeks used to do in New Athens. Even the girls."

Mike Latimer returned to his chair, bearing the glass. "Oh, yes. Your book about the communes. How's it going?"

"It's a real jazzer," Ted said glumly. He had half a mind to join the other in a drink.

Mike sipped at his brew. "You know, Ted, I think you've got a bad scene. If I were you, I'd get out from under like a goosed ballet dancer."

"Don't roach me. I wasn't so hot about the idea myself, but everybody else seems to be."

"Who's everybody else?"

"I told you about George Dollar. Well, yesterday the academician had me over to meet Henry Neville. You know, the local director of the National Security Forces. He's hot for it too."

Mike's eyes came up to Ted's face and there was a glint in them that hadn't been there before. He put down his glass, then put one hand over the back of the other and squeezed the knuckles.

"Henry Neville. Why in the hell should he be interested in your dissertation on communes?"

"What's wrong with Neville?" Ted said, frowning.

"I've run into him a dozen times. If this was fifty years ago, he'd be working with Senator Joe McCarthy."

"McCarthy?"

"Or, if it was sixty years ago, he'd probably take out German citizenship so he could enlist in Hitler's Gestapo."

"Oh, come on now. He's just a high-ranking cop."

"That's not his fault. Give him half a chance and he'd gladly start up a chain of concentration camps. Personally I hope he comes down with hardening of the urine."

Ted Swain decided he still didn't want anything alcoholic this time of the morning. It'd just make him loggy. However, he got to his feet and went into the kitchen for the cannister where he kept his hashish fudge. Only one piece left. He got it out and returned to the living room, nibbling on it.

He said to Mike, "The first time I ever met him. He seemed all right to me. Kind of down on the communes, is all. On the fanatical side about them."

"What did he want to know about the communes?"

"I gathered that his men had a hard time operating in commune country. The members refused to cooperate. He claims that they even shelter criminals, fugitives from justice."

Mike Latimer finished off his ale and snorted. "What criminals? How can you have any amount of crime when there is no money and nothing worth stealing that you couldn't get with your Universal Guaranteed Income?"

Ted Swain took another nibble at his fudge and said mildly, "There are crimes other than those involving stealing. Neville mentioned rape, for instance."

"Rape! In this day and age? Who wants to bother

100

with rape when all you have to do is tip your hat and say to just any girl at all, 'Wanta poke?' "

Ted laughed. "You're telling me. By the time I'm finished with this investigation, I'll be fucked flat. You don't have to ask them, they ask you ... if they take the time to ask. After I'm finished, remind me to give you a blow-by-blow description."

"Save me," Mike said. "What else did that funker Neville want to know?"

"Listen, don't use any of this on your program. With Dollar and Neville rooting for me, I've got it made. I don't want to antagonize them. If you said anything derogatory about either of them, they'd know your source."

"Wizard. But what else?"

"He's of the opinion that the communes are hotbeds of subversion, as he put it. He thinks they're potentially politically dangerous."

"Balls," the other snorted, coming to his feet. "So you've checked out two of these communes. What comes next?"

Ted Swain finished off the hashish fudge. He was already beginning to feel a slight high. "I guess I'll go over to Nature, the nudist commune. Then maybe Jissom, where they don't trust anybody over thirty, in the old tradition. I think I'll drive up to that farming commune, Walden, tomorrow. I haven't really gotten the feeling of this so far. I never paid any attention to the commune movement before; too busy with my studies to look around me."

"It's sweeping the country," Mike nodded. "I wouldn't be surprised if there weren't more of our population living in some sort of communes than otherwise." He waved his stick in a gesture of farewell. "Well, I guess I'll shirk off. See you, Ted."

"So long, hombre," Ted said to his back as the news commentator left.

He went on back into the kitchen. The hashish was getting to him and he felt like another piece. Two were about par for the course. If you took more, you were too high to operate. He fished in a drawer for his private recipe book.

He thought he'd try the El Majoun formula this time, direct from Morocco where they were specialists in the various manners in which to take cannabis. The Prophet had forbidden the faithful alcohol, but he hadn't said anything about kif, which was what they called marijuana in North Africa, and the Moslems had been taking the stuff just about universally ever since. He wondered why those who had taken such a dim view of cannabis here in the United States, back before it was legalized, hadn't considered the Arab countries before they viewed it with so much alarm. A dozen or more centuries of continual use seemingly hadn't hurt the followers of Islam.

Yes, here it was. El Majoun.

You took two pounds of almonds, browned in butter; one pound of walnuts; a handful of shelled acorns; two pounds of seeded raisins; a pinch each of black pepper, nutmeg, allspice and cinnamon; and pounded them together in a mortar until they were blended and then added one pound of honey and nine ounces of butter and cooked it all on a slow fire until it reached a thick, jamlike consistency. At this point you added an ounce or two of cannabis sativa and stirred well. You made the mixture into little balls about the size of a pecan and rolled them in sesame. And, yes, two of them were a sufficient dosage.

He went through the motions, noting that he was getting short on dates and acorns and reminding himself to get a new supply.

When he was finished he decided that he didn't want another piece, after all, and put his product in the ceramic cannister. He stood there for a moment, wondering whether or not he should whomp up some hashish marmalade while he was at it, but decided the hell with it.

As a matter of fact, he was only a moderate user of the stuff. He was usually too busy to want to blow his brains. And, for that, he understood that usage of cannabis had been falling off in recent years. Once it had been legalized, part of the fun of taking it had dropped away.

He went back into the study and looked glumly down at his voco-typer, library booster and auto-teacher. He didn't feel like doing the reports for Englebrecht. Possibly he'd do better, render them more interesting, if he had more data under his hat. He decided to drive over to Phoenecia and look up the nudist commune which Bat Hardin had mentioned.

He brought out his transceiver, summoned an electrosteamer, and headed for the door.

Nudist commune. Didn't they used to call them nudist colonies? From as far back as he could remember, he had heard the term, though he had never seen one. This must be one of the oldest types of communes, like-minded people who banded together so they could run around in common with others who desired to present themselves bare-assed. There was a considerable amount of near nudity, even full nudity on some beaches, these days, but he assumed that there were enough of the older generations around to voice objection to all-out nudity on the streets in everyday life.

The automated vehicle slithered up to the curb before him and he cocked a leg over the side and settled down behind the manual controls.

The road from West Hurley to Phoenecia took him through that part of the Catskills which he had been in the day before, through Lake Hill and past the turn-off road for New Athens. He loved the look and texture of the countryside. He enjoyed the sunlight breaking through nets of brilliant autumn leaves, and dancing about on the surface of the road like shiny new pennies. The sloping meadows were largely unmarred by houses or barns and occasional small lakes winked in the sunlight. It was a superlative day, he decided.

There was no difficulty in locating Nature. A dirt road branched off to it, before he reached the outskirts of Phoenecia. There was a large sign:

NATURE

NUDIST COMMUNE

WELCOME

It was narrow, the trees crowding in on each side, fallen red maple leaves paving it to such an extent that the gravel of the road was seldom seen.

He passed his first nudists before ever reaching the settlement proper; two women and a man strolling along in their birthday suits, obviously out to take in the beauty of the season. Middle-aged, the man had a paunch, the women, somewhat fallen breasts. They waved to him as he passed; he waved back.

There was no fence surrounding the commune but on its outskirts were what he assumed were the administration buildings. Three of them in all.

Another sign:

VISITORS WELCOME

PLEASE REGISTER HERE

Ted Swain parked his car and took the plunge.

The doors of the larger of the three buildings were open. He entered. In the empty hall beyond, another sign said *Visitors*, and there was an arrow pointing the way.

So he followed directions. Two doors down was one with another *Visitors* sign. The door was closed but he assumed the thing to do was to just walk in. He just walked in.

It was an informal office. Several chairs, a table with various magazines on it, all of a nudist nature, a largish couch, a small desk with nothing on it save a TV phone. One occupant stood at the window, her back to him.

Ted Swain cleared his throat and said, "Pardon me."

She turned, smiling.

104

Ted looked her over. It was a pleasure to do so. She wasn't twenty-five, although this was the year it could happen. An oval face, with the skin a little too tightly drawn over the bone underneath so that small hollows formed under high cheekbones. The skin itself was quite tanned, her hair the color of a gold miner's watch charm and worn in a carefully careless bob at the voguish length.

And she was dressed in the height of Nature fashion. In short, she was completely nude, down to and including delicately shaped feet. And Ted Swain was a foot man from way back. However, getting down to the feet covered a lot of admirable territory.

She obviously didn't give a damn about his eyes lingering over her navel, her femininely rounded tummy and the soft thatch of straw-colored pubic hair which celebrated her mons veneris. She continued to smile and said, "Could I help you?"

He could have replied differently to that, even though he told himself only a few hours earlier that Terpsichore, guide girl of New Athens, had rung him out like a dishcloth the day before. But he said, "I heard about Nature and thought I'd like to find out a little more about the razzle here."

"Of course." She approached and held out a hand for a shake. "I'm Bethie McBride. I'm receptionist today. Were you thinking of joining?"

Her hand was exactly what he could have expected it to be. The soft, dimpled, dry, warm hand of one of the most attractive girls he could offhand remember having met. If there hadn't been Sue Benny Voss, there in New Woodstock, the other day, he might have dubbed Bethie McBride *the* most attractive girl he had ever met.

He said, "Why ... I don't know. I just came to take a look."

He cleared his throat again. "That is ..."

She laughed pleasantly, sincerely and without throwing back her head to do it.

She said, "After the first few years in a nudist com-

105

mune you stop minding being looked at." She twisted her mouth in humor. "In fact, you're a bit miffed if a young male such as yourself doesn't look. Won't you sit down?"

She took her own place behind the desk and Ted selected one of the chairs. Only the top of her torso was now visible, unfortunately, so far as he was concerned.

He said, "In actuality, I'm a student over at the university city. I'm attempting to do a dissertation on the commune, on communes of all types. Nature is one of the closest to where I live. I thought I'd drop in and see what makes you tick."

"Of course. We nudists proselytize. Our ultimate aim is to convert the entire population of the country."

"Wouldn't that get a lot of opposition on the part of the Textile Guild?"

She laughed again. "Possibly. However, our present society has been eliminating unnecessary labor for decades, now. Work is a curse, not a blessing. Whatever happened to truck and bus drivers, now that we have automated vehicles?"

"They're all on Universal Guaranteed Income," he said. "By the way, my name's Theodore Swain."

He thought he detected a slight narrowing of her eyes at that, but he decided it couldn't be. Certainly she could never have heard of him before.

She said, "Ted, undoubtedly."

"Of course."

She said, "I'll be glad to show you around Nature. There's just one provision."

"Oh? What?"

"You'll have to remove your clothes."

He thought about that for an uncomfortable moment. "I'm afraid that might be embarrassing."

She said, "But why? On the face of it, everyone else is nude. If you weren't, you'd be as conspicuous as a walrus in a goldfish bowl."

He rubbed the back of his hand over his mouth and decided that in this atmosphere one couldn't be coy. He said, "The fact of the matter is, I'm ... uhh ... ab-

106

normally human. When I see a nude, pretty girl, I get an erection and I have a sneaking suspicion that you've got quite a few nude pretty girls around this commune."

"Why, yes." She smiled, a touch of the demure there. "But that's not to be worried about. What greater compliment could you pay a girl?"

He had never thought of it that way. His conservative family background was still with him to a certain extent.

"You mean . . ."

"Of course. None of our feminine members would object to you indicating that you thought them attractive. On the face of it, we are not prudes here in Nature, Mr. Swain. This commune was formed with the intention of eliminating prudery."

"I see." Ted Swain took a deep breath. "Wizard. Where do I leave my clothes?"

"Right in the closet over there."

"Where do I undress?"

"Why, right here."

"Wizard," he said, coming to his feet.

He turned his back to her and she smirked as he began to remove the bushjacket he wore, his kilts and shoes and socks. He hung them in the closet and then turned and looked at her, straight into her clear eyes.

"Prepare to be complimented," he said.

She blinked at him and tried to finance a smile that was bankrupt before it was born.

"I see what you mean," she said ruefully. "I suppose it wouldn't do for you to go about town looking quite so . . . aggressive."

"I told you," Ted said reasonably.

"Hmmm. Well, we'll have to do something about that, I suppose."

Chapter Twelve

"Such as what?" he said.

She took him by the hand and led him to the brown leather-covered couch and sat him down. He blinked somberly, awaiting developments.

They came immediately. She straddled him, with her hand helped him to enter, then settled down entirely. She smiled into his eyes.

"Did anyone ever tell you you were so ugly as to be handsome?"

He took a deep breath. "Not exactly. They usually tell me I look like Abe Lincoln."

She began gentle motion. "Well, you do. Have you ever seen the Brady portraits? That infinite sadness. I imagine Christ used to look like that."

"Jesus," he said meaninglessly. "Me?"

It seemed a hell of a conversation to be having under the circumstances. In actuality, the position had its advantages. You didn't have to worry about the girl. She was in command of the situation. It was also handy for kissing, and her full mouth had been designed for just that. He kissed her. Her tongue told him, without talking, that she wasn't inexperienced in that field either.

Her breath was beginning to come slightly faster.

He said, "Suppose somebody came in?"

Her breath was coming still faster, as was her move-

108

ment. "They could watch, or, if they wanted, join us."

Suddenly, her face went wan, her eyes vague and she excitedly bleated something he didn't get She stiffened, rammed herself violently against him a half dozen times. She slowed down, but didn't stop.

"Wow," she said.

She seemed an expert at multiple orgasm and came to climax twice more before they finished together. She remained where she was for a full couple of minutes before sliding from his diminished eminence to collapse back on the couch beside him.

She breathed deeply. "Is that better?"

He kept his fingers crossed as he remembered Sue Benny and said, "It's better than any I've had for a long time."

She twinkled her eyes at him mischievously. "I'll bet you say that to all the girls."

He said, "Well, are we ready to go out on the town?"

She thought about that, turned her head to look at him and he saw that her eyes were strangely clear and bright again. Bethie obviously loved the act of love.

She said, "I doubt it. I suspect that you're the virile type. Particularly with this in your mind, the first couple of girls you spotted and junior would be standing to rigid attention again. Wait a few minutes until I catch my breath."

"With these tactics," he said, "you must make a lot of converts to nudism."

"Oh, all visitors aren't like you."

"They couldn't be. You'd never stand up to it."

After a few minutes of mutual deep breathing, she reached over and began to caress him, and almost immediately he began to respond.

"See, I told you," she said.

He said hoarsely, "This time let me get on top. It drives me drivel-happy, not being able to move, especially right at the last."

"Wizard, hombre."

Later, they showered in the small bath that adjoined

109

the visitors' reception room, preparatory to going out to see Nature. Otherwise, the scent of spent sex would have notified one and all what they had been up to.

They left the reception building and strolled down the walk together, rounded the building and headed into the spread out town.

Ted Swain said, "That bit of razzle about someone coming in and either watching or joining us. What spins? Did you really mean it?"

"Of course."

"Well, what kind of sexual mores do you have here in Nature?"

"We don't have any. Long since, we in the nudist communes divorced ourselves from sex mores. They're ridiculous."

"They've been with us a long time, in spite of the way they're falling off these days," he said in mild protest.

"No they haven't. Have you ever heard of the illustration of man in the past 50,000 years having gone through approximately 800 lifetimes?"

"I don't believe so."

"Well, of those 800 lifetimes, at least 650 of them were spent in the caves. The caveman was a nudist, only donning the furs of animals when weather demanded it. And he had no such institution as marriage, or the pairing family. He was completely promiscuous. In the early clan system, all women were married, if you could call it that, to all the men."

"As an ethnologist, I'll accept that, although some wouldn't. The earliest forms of the family, the Consanguine and Punaluan were considerably dealt with by Lewis H. Morgan."

"Even the Egyptians were largely nudists, which isn't surprising in that climate," she said "Such things as clothing for the sake of modesty, rather than protection from the elements, didn't come in until organized religion. Neither did marriage. As a matter of fact, even today in many of the underdeveloped countries, the children go about nude until they reach puberty. And

110

even today there are no sex restrictions until marriage, and often not then."

"All right, so clothing and sex mores are comparatively recent in human history. But let's get to the present. You mean everybody pokes everybody in this commune?"

"Of course not. But you have sex with anybody you want to have it with."

"Wizard. Suppose somebody wants to poke you, but he doesn't particularly attract you. What happens?"

"Why, I suppose he'd find somebody else."

They were beginning to come up to some of the outlying homes of the community. So far as Ted Swain could see, the town was quite similar to West Hurley. The houses were of about the same size, nature and quality, and quite spread apart. The big difference was that all pedestrians were nude. And the kids playing in the street, as well. At least he had to admit they all had fabulous tans.

He looked at her and said, "Suppose this funker thought you the mopsy to end all mopsys. Really hot to get into your pants. No, obviously that's wrong. Really hot to get into you, period."

She quirked a smile. "Then I'd probably let him, out of pure kindness, poor fellow."

Ted Swain shook his head. "There must be a lot of poking going on in Nature."

"Of course. It's the greatest of all human pleasures, why not take advantage of the fact?" She pointed. "Now over there is our complex of swimming pools. Hot pools, cold pools, pools for the adults only, pools for children only, mixed pools, pools for athletes' practicing. We adore water, as we do sun."

He took in the extensive tennis courts and other facilities for sports. "Reminds me of New Athens, down near Lake Hill," he said.

"Oh, yes. We have a lot in common. They have quite a bit of nudism there; we have a good deal of sport here. We're trying to convert them to more nudism, they're trying to make us more Grecian." She laughed.

She easily laughed, he found. "The same goes on all over the country; the nudists trying to bring the Greek revivalists around, and they in turn trying to bring us around."

They were coming up on a fairly large park; gardens, lawns, trees, walks, benches, a pavilion in the center.

She said, "This is the plaza. The senior citizens, in particular, sit around and play chess, checkers, or cards, or whatever. We all spend as much time out in the sun as we can."

They strolled down one of the walks. There must have been several hundred oldsters on the benches, or sprawled on the grass. Admittedly, Ted decided, the human body is attractive only in youth. But he supposed that that applied to most other animals as well.

Bethie McBride said, "Now here is one of our original commune members. Perhaps you'll find him interesting to talk to. He's been here since before I was born."

They came up on a man sitting in complete relaxation upon a wooden bench. He could have been anywhere from seventy to ninety, Ted decided, and was tanned to Indian tone from feet to completely bald head. Withal, his paunch was but moderate and he seemed in excellent health. He was of medium height with a build that had started out to be fat and ended up as heavy-set. His face was round and inclined to puffiness about the eyes and under the chin. There were wrinkles at the corners of his eyes and a few near his mouth, but not nearly the number called for by his age. His beard was huge and gray, giving him a look something like a bald Karl Marx.

Bethie said in friendly tone, "Digger, here's a visitor. He's researching the communes, including Nature. I told him that if anybody could answer his questions, you could. His name is Ted."

Digger extended a hand in welcome. "Right on, Ted," he said. "Rest it." He gestured to the bench.

Ted sat, but Bethie McBride looked up at the sun

112

and said, "I'd better shirk off to the office. Some new visitors might turn up." She looked at Ted Swain and touched his cheek with the back of her hand. "I'll leave you with Digger. It will be lunch in an hour. I'll meet you at the autocafeteria."

He said, "Wizard." He couldn't help noting that everything about her seemed glowing, blond hair and blue eyes, smooth bare arms, shoulders, legs and body. All of it shining and precious in the autumn sunlight. She made a good ad for nudism.

She smiled again, her small quick smile, and turned and walked away, the way they had come.

The old man looked after her. "Dig that beautiful piece of ass. Really way out," he said definitely.

Ted wondered inwardly whether Digger was saying the girl was a good poke, or simply that her buttocks, admittedly unsurpassable, were beautiful to watch. Surely a girl in her twenties didn't put out for an oldster like this, even assuming the other was up to it.

Ted Swain put his arms on the back of the bench and relaxed. He said, "Bethie said you were the oldest of the commune members."

"Right, man. I'm the old pro, hereabouts."

"Do you mind telling me why you've chosen a nudist commune rather than some other type?"

"To watch the chicks, like. Can't do much more, these days, except maybe go down on them, like." He stirred in interest. "Look at the tits on that one. Groovy, heh? Wow."

Ted Swain looked at the passerby and inwardly agreed, though Bethie had left him in such shape that he couldn't thoroughly appreciate the woman walking by.

"How many years have you been involved in the communes?"

"Since forever, man. I was in it before the hippies came along. Like, in my day we called ourselves 'beatniks.' "

"Beatniks?"

113

"The beat generation. That's me, man." The old boy sighed. "We dropped out and most of us stayed out."

Ted Swain was beyond his depth. He said, "I haven't heard the word 'hippie' for a long time."

"Came from 'hep'. Hep to the jive. Meant you dug it."

Ted cleared his throat. "What was that term 'chick'?"

"Chick, chick. In my old man's day they called them broads, tomatoes. We called the young chicks teeny-boppers, for a while. I go way back, man. I dropped out before you were born."

"You mean you've been living in communes for more than thirty years?"

"Right on. Man, I was blasting tea back when you were still pissing in your diapers."

"Blasting tea?"

"You still call it pot, right? Right. When I was a kid, we used to call a joint a reefer. Called it a stick, later on. Reefers, muggles, doobies, weed, tea, grass, now pot. Pot's hung on for a long time. Like, when so many cats started using it, the name kind of froze."

"Uh, to go back a ways. This isn't really the first commune you've belonged to?"

The other looked at him in mild indignation. "Man, I've been, like, living in communes since I was a teenager. Back in Haight-Ashbury, back in Taos, back in San Miguel Allende, in Mexico. Weed was so cheap in Mexico it was practically free. Trouble was, the narks would bust you at the drop of a sombrero."

He thought back. "Taos was good. Real cool town when we first went there. We had three adobe pads like, up near Arroyo Seco, about eight miles out of town and bordering the Indian reservation. Right in the foothills of the Sangre de Cristo mountains, like. About twenty-five of us on an average. They'd come and go. We had gardens and chickens, and usually a few pigs."

"Sounds wizard. How did it work out?" Ted said, interested. "The farming, I mean. Were you able to raise all your own food? But, even if you did, how about clothes, gasoline for your cars, medicine, things like that? Were you able to sell some of your products?"

"No way, man. None of us were really farmers. We weren't behind the farmer scene. Got a few books and some of the government pamphlets but they didn't do us much good. Besides that, only five or six of us at a time ever really did much work. Most were more inclined to sit around and dig the guitars, or get high on grass. Threads? We didn't wear much in the way of threads; denims and khaki army shirts, like, mostly, and most of the year we went barefooted."

"But you had to have some money, for medicine and that sort of thing."

The other's square hands locked loosely across his slight paunch as he thought back. "Well, like, we played it cool. We just let the happening happen and then we took care of it the best we could, like. From time to time, somebody'd join up with us that had a little bread. Money from the squares at home, maybe. They'd toss it into the kitty. We'd scrounge around, shine on some of the neighbors, or down in town. Sometimes, not often, we'd have some cat with us with itchy fingers. Maybe he'd rip off something and we'd flog it."

Ted Swain closed his eyes briefly and gave a short rapid shake of his head, as though incapable of quite assimilating this. He said, "But if your garden was a flop, what did you eat?"

"Man, you bring it all back to me, like," Digger said. "We had some stuff from the gardens, but mostly what we'd do is buy a sack of corn, or maybe barley or oats, when we had some bread to buy it with. Or there was one straight who owned a feed store and felt sorry for us. One of his own kids had taken off for Haight-Ashbury and he hadn't heard from the chick for more than a year. We'd send one of the chicks over, like, with one of the kids on her hip, and she'd shine him on and he'd spring with a sack of corn and we'd grind it up and make corn bread and mush. We got pretty good at panhandling too. And then they started the food-stamps bit

115

and we made that scene. The man issued these free food stamps and you got basic commodities the government had bought up as surplus, like. It was real cool."

"Suppose you got sick?"

"Well, we all hung in there together. Maybe one of us had some medic training in the army; maybe one of the chicks had studied nursing for a year or two before dropping out. If it was something, like, really bad, we'd split to the free clinic in Taos."

"None of you ever worked?"

"No way. Wow, dig this chick coming down the walk, man. Dig the sway of those hips."

The girl passed and grinned at the lecherous old devil. "Hi, Digger," she said. "What spins?"

Digger leered at her. "You know what I'd like to make spin."

"Get goosed, padre," she grinned at him. She looked Ted Swain up and down before passing on. She couldn't have been more than eighteen or twenty and had red hair and green eyes, and her brush of pubic hair was red as well. Ted couldn't remember ever having poked a redhead. He reminded himself to look into the matter, though after his experiences of the past few days he had about as much interest in sex as a hermit.

He sighed and went back to the aged hippy. "How did you pay the rent for your houses and land if you had no source of income?"

"See if I can remember the scene. Oh, yeah. Like, one of the chicks had a rich father. Before she dropped out, she ripped off a couple of grand. Wrote some bummer checks or something. Anyway, when she joined up with us, she still had some of the bread. Put five bills into the kitty and we bought three acres of land and the three adobes. They weren't much in the way of pads. Dirt floors, no electricity, homemade furniture, no water. We had to haul the water in garbage cans from the spring. Had an outhouse. Man, did it stink."

Ted Swain couldn't visualize it very well. He said, "But where'd you get money for gasoline?"

"We didn't have any wheels. If we wanted to go somewhere, we thumb tripped."

"You mentioned children. Were any of you married?"

Digger thought back, scratching himself on the stomach. "I don't believe so. We usually had three or four kids around. Everybody took care of them. Sometimes we'd forget who they belonged to. Maybe some chick'd split and leave her kid behind. We'd keep care of it. Maybe one of the other chicks, or maybe one of the cats, would kind of adopt it. Everybody dug kids."

Ted Swain wished he had his electronic bug. He would have liked to have recorded this. It was all new to him. He had been born in the '60s of a moderately well-to-do Wasp family. His parents were both college educated; his father a sales manager. Ted had never been exposed to the hippies. He hardly more than knew the word.

He said carefully, "You mentioned begging and even petty thievery. Didn't the local authorities take a dim view of you?"

Digger shifted his position a bit. "Oh, once in a while we'd get into a heavy scene. Maybe one or two of us would get busted. Maybe for possession, or whatever. We used to blow grass and take any other stuff we could get, speed, hash. But we just played it cool, like. A couple of months in the slammer never hurt anybody. At least you'd get a few square meals, and when they turned you out, they'd usually give you some threads."

"How about the local people, the, uhh, squares?"

"They were all right, like, at first. It was the chicano kids, mostly, that didn't dig us. Man, they all had the straight dream, like. They wanted to get good jobs, wheels, a color idiot box. They couldn't get behind the scene, like. They couldn't dig the fact that we were in a position to get all that jazz, and didn't. Some of us, most of us, came from pretty good families, like. Most of us had a little college. Some of us had pretty good

117

jobs before dropping out. Man, they couldn't see it, no way. So once in a while we'd have a rumble on our hands, if we went on into Taos. Once a half dozen of them cornered a couple of our chicks and gang-banged them." The oldster chuckled. "Like, if they'd known how far out those two chicks were, they wouldn't have had to get rough."

Ted Swain hesitated. "How were you all politically?"

"Politics? Man, that wasn't our scene. We'd really dropped out, like. Oh, we used to dig the demonstrations when we were in Haight-Ashbury. Go over to Berkeley, and all that jazz. Peace marches, and that bit. But, man, Taos was squaresville."

"What finally happened?"

"What happened? Man, you're really not with it. Guaranteed Annual Income happened. They call it Universal Guaranteed Income now. Man, like all of a sudden we all had it made. It wasn't much bread, at first, but it was enough to get by on in a commune. They started springing up all over the place, like. And every election went by, the politicians upped the ante. And with automation, and then ultramation, coming along, there were less and less jobs, like, and more and more dropouts. That was when the communes really start booming, like."

A gleam came to rheumy eyes. "Look at that young chick playing on the grass. Man, she's only about eleven years old, but the way she's going, in two years she'll have tits the size of cantaloupes. Hope I live to see it."

Chapter Thirteen

By the time he drove away from Nature, he was believing as much in this dissertation of his as he did in purple leprechauns. He could see, perhaps, doing an article on the modern commune, something to appear as a paper to be presented for fellow ethnologists. But a book length of, say, 60,000 words or more? He just couldn't believe he could find that much material, no matter how many communes he visited. For one thing, they were too similar. Oh, there were surface differences, one was nudist, one composed of Greek revival sport fans, one a mobile art colony. But, in actuality, beneath the surface, they were considerably alike.

After his session with the sex-obsessed old man, Digger, he had rejoined Bethie McBride and they had gone to the town's autocafeteria where he'd sat at the table with Nature's mayor—or whatever they called him—and one member of the city council. Their positions were not official. Nature didn't bother to participate in the politics of the vicinity. They had no interest even in regional senators, nor in the Presidential elections, not to speak of county officers. They were a unit within themselves, and paid as little attention as possible to the outside world.

Their life was by no means austere. They obviously

used up their collective Universal Guaranteed Income on maintaining as high a standard of living as possible. Those who had been selected on job-muster day commuted to their jobs, donning clothes, and returning to the Sybaritic life when their stint was over. Those who had no employment, seldom left it.

They were vegetarians, teetotalers and abstained from any narcotics, even tobacco and caffeine, and made a great to-do about nutrition and health, exercise and bodybuilding, almost as much so as the members of New Athens, but some of them seemed to have other interests as well. Some practiced one or another of the arts, some studied one or more of the sciences, literature, the humanities, or whatever. Some tinkered in amateur machine shops. Several ran an old-fashioned press, setting their own type, even making their own paper. They printed their own books and a tabloid-size paper devoted to Nature.

As a matter of fact, Ted Swain could see himself joining such a commune, if he wasn't so tied up in his efforts to obtain his degree and step into teaching. It could be a full life, he was convinced.

Henry Neville came to his mind. What could he possibly report that would interest Neville? George Dollar, of the National Data Banks, yes. Anything he discovered at all would be grist for the data-banks mill. But Neville? These people weren't interested in politics, not to speak of subversion, and certainly he doubted if there were any criminal fugitives hiding out in Nature. They simply weren't the criminal type. The same thing applied to New Athens.

The hour was still moderately young. He should have time for a quick visit to one more commune. He looked at his list. At Nature they had given him a roll of nudist communes throughout United America. There were evidently as many of them as those devoted to the Greek revival theme. Ted Swain had no idea at all, as recently as a few days ago, of the existence of either. If nothing else came of this brainstorm of

Englebrecht's, he decided gloomily, he was learning something of the workings of his country.

Jissom, he decided. What a name for a commune! It was near Bearsville. Which, in turn, was just beyond Lake Hill. This whole area seemed combed with communes. He wondered if the whole country was. It must be. Somebody had said that possibly half the population of the nation lived in some type of commune. What did he know about Jissom? Practically nothing. Nobody over the age of thirty, which eliminated him. And they were adherents of the drug culture, whatever that was. Hadn't somebody said something about their bringing up mushrooms from Mexico, or coca from Peru?

It was getting later than he had thought. He drove back through the village of Lake Hill; small, a town of yesteryear. He turned on his headlights. The darkness was settling swiftly. Where the mountains had been a mass of color, they were now purple and black, and the shadows were out, pushing the last diffused rays of light over the horizon.

He looked up the coordinates of Bearsville and punched them into the autodrive and stretched out his legs and put his head back as a bone-deep weariness seeped through his body. He was mentally, physically, and, face it, sexually weary. How long had he been on this? Only three days?

Bearsville was a little larger than Lake Hill, and old-fashioned. He wondered if it was some sort of commune, people who held onto a vanishing past. He wouldn't bother to inquire right now, possibly later. The houses kept the traditions of the past; wooden, New England style, painted white. He asked a passerby for directions, and, in manual control again, headed up a side road.

Jissom was so near to Bearsville that had either of the towns added a few dozen houses they would have merged. And it came back to him, all over again, how similar these communes were. You could have driven through most of them without ever thinking of it as

121

anything other than an ordinary village or town. Well, that wouldn't apply to Nature, of course, where a few acres of bare skin were on display, and in New Athens the Greek costume and the temple in the center of town would tip you off. But Lesbos and Jissom were almost identical to West Hurley, though he still couldn't really think of his community as a commune.

What in the hell *was* a commune? Seemingly, the basic factor was a gathering of people who had deeply felt common interests, as opposed to an ordinary community in which the citizens went to hell in their own way. Most of them seemed to merge their incomes into a community fund upon which all drew to the extent needed. To paraphrase the old slogan he had thought of before, from each his Universal Guaranteed Income, to each according to his needs. Of course, that didn't apply to West Hurley. Each individual there kept his own credit account and only when some community project such as a swimming pool or a golf course was voted in did each resident contribute his share.

Well, here was Jissom. If it conformed to the usual set-up of the communes, there would be some sort of community building, or buildings. And, yes, there in the more-or-less center of the several hundred houses were two large two-storied buildings, the only structures of more than one floor in the vicinity. Over one of them was a simple sign, JISSOM.

He parked his electrosteamer before it, shook off his weariness and emerged to look up and down the streets. There was a fair amount of pedestrian traffic, male and female, all attired as he would have expected in West Hurley, informally and in a score of styles. The only difference between this and his own town was that the average age was at least ten years younger. West Hurley made no strong point about it but so far as Ted Swain could remember, the oldest resident must have been Jim Hawkins, who was in his early forties. Someone had told him that Jissom drew the line at thirty. He wondered what happened when someone hit his thirty-first birthday. Did they run him, or her, out of town?

He made his way to what he assumed to be the town hall, or whatever they called it. The doors opened before him as he approached.

Some town hall. The front doors opened into an enormous barroom dimly lit, a long automated bar extended along the wall facing the entry. More than fifty stools lined it. There were tables with chairs, haphazardly strewing the floor, leaving room only for a sizable dance space. Couches, some of them as large as king-size beds, lined most of the walls. Some of the wall space was made up of booths. Wall decorations were in a shocking psychedelic rage of color and the canned music was deafening. Ted Swain didn't recognize it but Ted Swain was no connoisseur of music; his own simple tastes tended toward folk.

The place was packed with at least a couple of hundred on the dance floor, usually paired, but not necessarily so; both male and female singles were dancing, some of them obviously drunk—or high. There were couples on most of the couches, but it was too dim to make out what they were doing. The fumes of pot were so all embracing that Ted suspected one could get high by doing no more than remaining in the room for an hour or so.

He stood a few yards inside the door and looked about hesitantly.

At a table nearby a girl sat alone, smoking. She was nobody's pin-up. Lifeless brown hair drawn severely back into a bun at the nape of a short, thick neck, sallow skin, mismatched features and a figure with too many pounds in the wrong places. Possibly about twenty-five, though she could have passed for thirty-five without much effort.

Ted approached and said, "I beg your pardon but . . ."

She eyed him out of a face filled with nothing at all. She slurred, "Goose off, padre."

He said, "I only wanted to ask . . ."

123

Her eyes were opaque. She was obviously higher than a satellite. "Get spayed," she muttered and looked away, dragging on the joint which she held loosely in her left hand.

A voice from behind him said, "You wanted something, hombre?"

Ted turned.

The newcomer had a cold, narrow face and theatrically long black hair which flowed back from his forehead in carefully sculpted waves. Surprisingly, considering his obvious youth, he had wings of gray at his temples, silvery against his dark, flushed cheekbones. He was in his late twenties, Ted guessed, but it appeared that he had ridden through those years at a full, frantic gallop; his eyes were staring and strange, with a milky shine like that of a trachoma victim and he seemed to be boiling inwardly with hostility. Ted Swain hadn't the slightest idea why.

Ted said, "I'm a stranger. I come from West Hurley, a . . . a commune over toward Kingston. I heard about Jissom and thought I'd give it a look."

"Verily," the other sneered, "your words resemble the excretion of the male bovine. If you've heard anything at all about Jissom, you know fucking well we don't allow anybody over thirty."

Ted said reasonably, "I didn't say I wanted to join, only that I thought I'd give you a look."

"Why, padre? You don't look as though you're the far-out type, and this commune's as far out as you can get without beginning to come back."

Ted said, "Actually, I'm over at the university city and I'm working on a dissertation about communes." He couldn't understand the other's hostility. If strangers weren't welcome in Jissom, why not just say so and ask him to leave?

"Oh, you are, eh?" The other jerked his head and two other youths, stocky types with a dangerous air, materialized at each side of Ted Swain. They seemed to be on something too but he wasn't sure if it was only pot, or not.

124

The first one said, "Come along," and led the way, zigzagging between chairs and tables.

Ted supposed that he should have balked and retreated to his car but the whole situation was so irritating that he followed, just to see what was happening. The two others came closely behind. He wondered if they would let him go, even if he wished. What was the scenario, anyway?

At the far end of the pulsing nightclub—that could be the only word for it—a door opened upon their approach. The four of them passed on through into a hallway from which doors opened off to the left and right. It looked like nothing so much as a standard office building, slightly run down. The door closed behind them, obviously soundproof since the din of the nightclub suddenly fell away completely.

The leader said nothing, continuing to show the way. He opened the third door and they filed in. Ted Swain had expected an office, but it wasn't. The room held several couches, a low table, several leather comfort chairs. There were no windows, the lighting was indirect and the wall-to-wall carpeting was the thickest he could ever remember having seen. The walls were leather padded to the height of some five feet and there was a TV screen on one of them. There were no paintings or other decorations.

The leader grated, "Sit down, padre." He himself took one of the heavy chairs, but the two goon-types remained standing, near the door.

Ted sat down and said, attempting to keep his voice even, "What spins, hombre? By the way, my name's Doctor Theodore Swain." He added the "doctor" bit in hopes of realizing a little prestige with these obviously less than intellectual types.

The other's eyes narrowed. "Oh, it is, eh? I've heard about you, you fink."

Ted Swain stared at him. "Fink?" he said.

"We know all about your demibuttocked prying into the communes for that shit-assed Neville and that crook Dollar."

125

"Look here," Ted scowled, "you're not reading the script. I'm not working for Neville and Dollar. I'm working for myself, under the lead of my director of dissertation, Academician Englebrecht."

A look of hesitancy came into the other's vague eyes. "Oh yeah?" He looked at one of his two burly, silent companions. "Jimmy, go get us some drinks. We'll look into this but nobody can say we're not hospitable here in Jissom." For some reason, he laughed at his own words.

Jimmy turned to the door and left.

The leader of the three said to Ted, "You can call me John, and this is Clark. Clark, frisk him. Stand up, Swain."

"Now look here . . ." Ted Swain began.

"How do we know you're not some sort of fruitcake, packing a shooter? There's a lot of funkers that think Jissom is a little *too* far out and think we ought to be abolished, one way or the other, and usually the other."

Ted shrugged and stood.

Clark went over him carefully. The electronic bug was pinned behind his jacket lapel. Clark grinned nastily at him and ripped it out and tossed it to the table in front of the man who called himself "John."

John looked at it coldly. "What's that?"

Ted said, "I record all the conversations I get into. That minimike sends it back to my study, where it's played out on a disk."

The other took up the bug, dropped it to the floor and ground it under his heel. It was done before Ted Swain could protest. Nevertheless, it wasn't overly important. He could easily get another one.

Jimmy re-entered the room with a tray holding four cocktail glasses. He handed them around, taking one himself.

Actually, Ted felt he could use a drink. Nature didn't believe in alcoholic beverages, being vegetarian and on its health kick, so he hadn't had anything that day.

John held up the glass in a sullen sort of toast. "Chug-a-lug," he said.

Ted Swain responded, "Cheers, cheers." And when the other knocked back his drink in one swallow, Ted followed suit.

The drink was on the strange side. Pleasant enough, but it didn't seem to be particularly alcoholic. Jimmy and Clark finished their own and put their empty glasses down on the table.

"We have about twenty minutes," John said in satisfaction.

"Twenty minutes until what?" Ted said, a suspicion beginning to grow.

"Twenty minutes until it *hits* you."

"What hits me?" Ted felt a prickly feeling along his spine and a lifting sensation to the hair on the back of his neck.

"The lysergic acid diethylamide, padre. Better known as LSD-25. You've just had 350 micrograms of it."

Ted had resumed his seat; now he rose again, in alarm. "I'm getting out of here."

Jimmy laughed. Clark grinned.

John said, "I wouldn't recommend it. You've got about twelve hours ahead of you, padre, in which you could kill yourself without even trying, or possibly kill somebody else. You're taking a trip, padre, if you want to or not. Your best bet is to stay right here where we can take care of you. We've been through this a hundred times over. None of us have taken anything. Only you. We'll help you get through it. The first time you get your ego smashed can be a pretty bad scene, a real jazzer."

Ted Swain licked his suddenly dry lips. "I've never had anything harder than hashish."

Clark grinned at him. "Acid isn't hard. It's not even stuff. You can't get hooked on it, even if you wanted to."

Ted darted a look of not understanding at John. "But, *why?*"

127

"Ever hear of truth serum?"

"You mean scopolamine?"

"There's others, too. Some better. But nothing so good as acid. Padre, a couple of hours from now and you'll answer any questions asked, and not give a damn that you're doing it, particularly in view of the fact that you'll realize that you love us, along with all the rest of the human race, with an undying love." John laughed a bitter laugh. "We'll find out all about your deal with Neville, every little detail of it."

"You're all drivel-happy," Ted snapped. "What do you think will happen when I report this to the National Security Forces?"

Jimmy said easily, "Who'd believe you?"

John said, "Now listen. It's going to hit you along in here, somewhere. There's a couple of things you want to remember. During the experience you're going to come to places where you have alternatives. When you reach them, imagine you can go upstream or down. Go downstream always, if you can. Just drift with it. Second, if you get hung up, trust us. In spite of what you think now, you can trust us on this trip of yours. If you feel that you're not able to hack it, call on us. We'll be here."

Clark said, "What kind of music do you like?"

"Music? Don't roach me."

"No joke. It's best to have background music. Listen, padre, you're on a trip now if you want to be or not. We'll see you through."

"I like folk music."

John snorted contempt but said, "So, get the flat some folk music, Jimmy."

Jimmy went over to the screen on the wall and dialed. Faint music flooded the room.

It started with a sour taste in his mouth and his vision began to become prismatic. There was a pressure in his head. The air crackled silently. He had the feeling of colored musical notes floating about, and the scene seemed like a Picasso drawing. He felt nauseated but it passed. The music was louder and the guitar strings beautifully separated.

The three were looking at him and he began to laugh. What a ridiculous, humorous thing. Why not, though? "Yes, why not?"

He must have said it aloud, because Clark said, "Why not, hombre?"

Ted Swain laughed. He couldn't stop. Everything he could think about was ridiculously and pitifully funny. The world. The universe. All the poor sweet ridiculous folks he knew. Himself. What a razzle. Filled with noble, ridiculous people. The whole universe. The universe!

The reaction, cosmic laughter, was different from any amusement he had ever before known. It came out as though propelled by a power much larger than himself. It came right up from the center of his psyche. It resembled both a mild and sustained electric shock passing through body and spirit, and a mild and incomplete continuing orgasm. A twisting and pulsing current which, for want of a fresh image, could be described as the life force shaking him, as if he might be aboard or bestride, or being carried along with, the force that penetrates and fills all beings.

He laughed and laughed.

He could hear John saying, "The ones who begin laughing always feel the terror after. They realize that the joke is on them."

Chapter Fourteen

He wept and sobbed, occasionally he chuckled. He felt sorry for himself as though he were someone else.

He made cries of despair. "Oh, heaven . . . this is terrible! I . . . I . . . I didn't know reality could be so physical. This stuff won't let you go. . . . Oh . . . my god, what have I done?"

He glared at John, Jimmy and Clark, who were all seated and watching him calmly. "Why are *you* so peaceful?" he demanded. "How can you sit there and smile while I suffer? Why am I the only one to suffer?" Then he added in a tiny voice, "I guess there are others. Lots of others. Everybody. They suffer as well."

"Yeah, hombre," Jimmy said consolingly.

Ted said, "This is terrible. God . . . I want to get back." He had forgotten that he was an agnostic with atheistic tendencies.

"Go along with it," one of them said, compassion in his voice. It was Clark. Ted could see him through air that seemed to have metamorphosed to liquid.

"Go along with it," Ted repeated. "Yeah, wizard. That's wizard. Ha! Ha! But it's hard. I wonder if I can stand up. Shall I try?" He no longer disliked them. Any of them. Even John. They were taking care of him, getting him through this.

"Sure, padre, try," Clark said.

Ted staggered erect and moved, wavering, around the padded room, through the knee-deep carpeting, banged up against the wall, gently, easily, flowingly.

"There, you see. I did it. I can walk. What's the point?"

They all laughed but then he heard strange music. "What's that? That's not folk. It's religious music. Is it real?"

"No," somebody said.

"I'm objectionable," Ted said. "So objectionable." He repeated it several times.

"Yeah, you are kind of a pain in the ass," John said.

He decided that he loved Sue Benny Voss and he wanted her. He wanted her in her entirety, not just to poke her. He wanted *her*.

The physical world he could see had begun to slowly come apart. No square inch of space had anything to do with any other. Everything in his field of vision seemed to turn into bright colored water. There was no time, no space, nothing but a flow. He waded through the room, making his way unsteadily. Around him the music and lights, the voices of the others, all combined and flowed. Yet he could see the three watching him and he saw his own situation with terrible clarity. He had gone too far and couldn't get back!

He called, "Save me. I want to return!"

The jelly before his eyes separated. The universe cracked into bright globules and separated; then he was in little pieces, about to no longer exist, and flowing away on something like a jet stream; this must be the stream John had mentioned—dear sweet John—stream of unconsciousness that one was supposed not to resist. Let the ego die. Go along with it. But he fought upstream all the way.

Clark caught his hand and said, "Flow along with it."

But Ted Swain rasped, "Get me out. I want to go home. Where is she?" Where was Sue Benny?

They were like people trying to help him in his en-

131

velope of flowing jelly, not being able to do anything but be compassionate.

"Help me return!"

Jimmy led him back to his chair and seated him. He said, "There's no way you can shorten this. You've got to go through every stage. You've got to go all the way. Just relax."

Where had the universe gone? He'd find it. He could fumble his way out!

He found himself on the floor, in the thick carpeting, rolling, shouting and sobbing. He could feel mucus running down from his nose; he reached up both hands and smeared it all over his face.

He felt the ego could stand against the universe for just so long and then it must let go and collapse, going downstream. But at some point there must occur the ride into the hell of ego, a passage through glowing coils which plant endless bright circles in the mind. Far from home, far into inner space, the voyager could no longer be helped by his companions who cruised compassionately alongside the frightened speck of ego. The compassionate hand is outstretched but ignored, and the ego travels in no time, no space, no dimension, like an astronaut flung out too far who will never return until time bends back on itself.

Meanwhile, the fleck of existence performed every act it had ever dreamed of performing. While the body constantly changed positions, during which, at various times, it was fetal, crawling and sucking its thumb, the speck was pushed by a tremulous current into a lotus of nude bodies, and, diving in, was folded into the cosmos, as if the cosmos was fucking itself. The speck then flew to the top of all things, and saw in every direction what was and will be.

In space an endless power station, plugged and electrical, with a current pulsing through every part of it. This structure, resembling a playground jungle gym, was the sum of all being. Individual living beings attached, in stasis, composed the structure. The relationship of each being to the cosmos was somehow religious and also sexual.

Thereafter the speck whirled down a great growing tract, experienced a terrific pressure, as if its mass were built up intolerably and re-entering was thrust down, labored, felt a collar, and burst clear of the ordeal.

He rested on the couch, with the colored musical notes still slithering around him, and he was shivering and saying, "I want to go home now. Where is Sue Benny?"

Jimmy had evidently left the room. John said, "You're only a third of the way through."

"No," Ted said. "I won't return there."

"It wouldn't be necessary," Clark said from a great distance. The death-and-rebirth phase was passed. Now he was on a plateau, the philosophical plateau from which he could take off again or come back down.

John said, "How do you feel, Doctor Swain?"

"It was terrible."

John said, "Now you know what it's like to suffer ego loss. And now tell me all about Henry Neville and George Dollar and what it was they wanted to know about the communes."

Ted Swain talked, talked and talked, the words seldom making much sense to him. From time to time John would ask another question. They didn't seem to make much sense, either.

Finally, John said to Clark, "Get him back to his car."

The younger man didn't like it. "You think he's able to drive?"

"What the shit do we care? It's like we heard. The funker's a fink. Get him out of here. If he busts his neck on the way home, what do we care?"

"Yeah, but suppose he busts somebody else's neck?"

However, Clark took the unresisting Ted Swain by the arm and helped him from the chair in which he was again seated. He conducted him to the door. The musical notes still jumped, the walls pulsated, but the small shudders of electricity were fading. He felt that

133

his whole life had come tumbling down and that he was sitting happily in the rubble. He wasn't distressed.

He had no memory of leaving the building, of being put into his car. He was still nervously crackling with energy. He couldn't remember how to dial the coordinates of his home in West Hurley, so he was driving manually. Somehow, he had gotten through Bearsville and was on the highway beyond. The car looked as holey as swiss cheese and the sides seemed to billow about him. The colored musical notes still floated by, but not so many of them. Small, throbbing currents still moved through his body, but he felt that he was coming down.

He regained control of himself to the point where he realized that he shouldn't be driving and pulled off to the side of the road and sat there, breathing deeply. He had no way of knowing how much longer the LSD-25 would affect him. He had no way of knowing how much time had elapsed since he had been given the stuff. What in the hell had gotten into him to take that drink, particularly in view of the hostility of John and the other two? He must have been drivel-happy. And the way he had put it down. Chug-a-lug, John had said, and down the whole thing went. How stupid could you get? A child would have suspected anything given to him in that atmosphere. Probably it didn't make any difference, however. There were three of them, all at least as good physical specimens as himself. They could have poured the drink down him, if they'd had to.

It must be nearly dawn. And, yes, even as he sat, his sense of time still distorted, the sky began to light. The rim of the sun had not as yet appeared on the horizon, but the eastern skies began to blaze with golden light; it was as if a majestic fire were raging below the edge of the world.

A car was approaching from the opposite direction. It slowed, came to a halt. The driver looked over at him.

"This is the road to Bearsville, isn't it?" he called. "I seem to have lost my regional map."

He was tall and thin with a great sprout of erratic red hair which seemed to require all of his body's strength to nourish; at least it was the only thing about him that looked strong and luxuriant. His ribs showed sharply against a sport shirt and there were great dark hollows beneath surprisingly bright gray eyes.

"Yes," Ted got out. "I forget how far."

The other squinted at him. "Are you all right?"

Ted got out, "No. No, I'm under the influence of LSD. Could you help me?"

The newcomer left his car and came over. He looked at Ted Swain narrowly. "LSD?" he said. "What are you doing out on the road like this, under LSD?"

"I . . . I guess it was kind of a gag. I . . . I didn't know I was taking it. Could you dial the coordinates of my home for me? I . . . I must have them somewhere in my wallet, or some place."

"They'll be on the cover of your transceiver. Why didn't you call for a medic car?"

Ted fumbled in his pockets for his transceiver. When he brought it forth, it too seemed full of holes. He handed it over. "If I'd called for a medic car, the Medical Guild would have reported to the National Security Forces that I had been on the roads under the influence of a drug."

The other made a sudden decision. "Listen, hombre," he said, "this is a bad scene for you. Dismiss this car and come over to mine. I'll take you home. You can't be left by yourself. I've seen folks under LSD before. You've still got a long way to go. You ought to be in bed."

Ted Swain would have taken orders from anyone who gave them. He got out of his electrosteamer. He said, "I've forgotten how to dismiss it."

The other did it for him, took Ted by the arm and escorted him to his own car. The sky was getting quite light. He got his charge into a seat, closed the door behind him and circled the vehicle to get into the driver's place.

"Some gag," he said. "Don't your practical-joke friends know that stuff's dangerous? It's potentially dangerous to anybody who takes it and to anybody in his vicinity. I know of a chap on a trip who got out into traffic and tried to hug an automated truck. Unfortunately, the truck was moving."

The musical notes were faint now, but to Ted the car too seemed full of holes.

The other said, "My name's Gerald Fry." He checked the coordinates of Ted's home, on the transceiver, then handed it back while he dialed them.

"Doctor Theodore Swain," Ted said. "I've got to thank you for all this trouble you're going to."

"Doctor?" Gerald Fry said. "And somebody hooked you into taking LSD?"

"Ph.D, not medical," Ted said as the car got underway. "Took my degree in ethnology."

"I'm a sociologist, myself," Fry said. "I'm still working for my doctorate."

"I've been trying to take my academician's for so long I can't remember," Ted told him.

"Is it as tough in these parts as it is in my neck of the woods to get an acceptable subject for your dissertation?"

They were zipping through the countryside, alone on the surface roads in the early morning. There were still some distortions, but Ted Swain knew he was coming out of it.

He said, "Yes, but I think that possibly I've now got one. I specialize in the ancient Aztecs. As you probably know, they had a communal society, based on the clan. My director of dissertation came up with the idea of my researching present-day communes and comparing them with ancient ones."

Gerald Fry looked at him. "You've got to be kidding."

Ted said defensively, "Well, I thought it was kind of

136

far out myself, but everybody else I talk to seems to think it's a real jazzer."

"No, that's not what I mean. It's just that that's what I'm doing for my doctorate. This is one hell of a coincidence, my meeting you."

Ted Swain stared at the other, wondering if the LSD were still affecting him. "Now look, hombre, don't roach me. You mean to tell me that you're doing a dissertation on a comparison of ancient and modern communes?"

"No. I'm doing a work on the drug-culture communes. Takes me all over the country. I'm from the university city just south of Denver—University City 111."

They were pulling into West Hurley; the car slowed and maneuvered itself down the streets, to come up before Ted's house. West Hurley was devoid of either pedestrian or vehicular traffic.

Gerald Fry said, "I'd better come in with you. I suspect you have at least a couple of hours to go. LSD can hang on beyond the point where you think you're all right."

"Wizard," Ted Swain said. "Let's have some breakfast. I'm starved." He led the way into the house. The door's identity screen registered him and opened up.

Inside, Fry ran a hand through already mussed red hair. He said, "I still say it's a real jazzer that we met."

Ted Swain showed him into the kitchen-dining room. "Not as much as all that. Were you heading for Jissom?"

Fry wedged himself into the alcove containing the room's sole table. "How did you know?"

"That's where I got my slug of LSD. I was there for the same purpose you were. Investigating the communes. They didn't want to be investigated."

He brought out his filter outfit for making coffee, and went to work with it. So far as he was concerned, he seemed to be perfectly all right. Fry evidently thought he needed a couple of more hours of supervision but aside from a little music in his ears, he

137

couldn't see why. It must have been a full twelve hours ago that he had taken his dosage.

Gerald Fry looked at him. "What didn't they want to be investigated?"

"I'll be a funker if I know. They never told me. They seemed to know about me, that Henry Neville and George Dollar were interested in my findings. I couldn't read the script. Bunch of weirds."

"Who're Neville and Dollar?"

"This region's National Security Forces head and this region's National Data Banks director."

Fry's expression was serious; his eyes were narrowed and there was a strange frown on his forehead. "This is going to roach you, but, you know, the same applies to me in Denver."

"How do you mean?" Ted Swain went on with the coffee. The handle of the coffee pot seemed to droop, as though in a Dali surrealistic painting, but otherwise his trip seemed to be about over.

"It mean the heads of both the data banks and security out there thought my project was a real razzle."

Ted brought the coffee to the table, along with pseudocream and saccharin. He said, "Dial anything you want to eat. I'm an amateur cook but I'm not up to it now. Maybe it's understandable."

The other fixed his cup of coffee the way he wanted it. "This is all I need. Too early to eat. I got my time table mixed up or I wouldn't have been around at this Zoroaster of an hour. What's understandable?"

Ted Swain was ravenously hungry. He hadn't eaten the evening before and since then had spent an exhausting twelve hours. In fact, he couldn't remember ever having been so wrung out. He dialed a whale steak and a baked potato and poured himself coffee while he waited.

He said to his companion seated across the table, "That the National Security Forces and the data banks would be interested in what you discover in the com-

138

munes in your part of the country, just as they are here."

"Yeah, but the thing is, we're not alone. I met another postgraduate student poking into the communes."

Ted Swain eyed him. "You did? Is everybody trying to get into the act? What was his bit?"

The redhead ran a nervous hand back through his thatch and frowned. "He was doing a paper on crime in the communes and how they handled it. Many of them avoid the National Security cops, you know. They have their own law enforcement. He wasn't getting much cooperation. The tendency was to clam up and tell him to shirk off. They claimed they didn't have any crime."

Ted said, "Well, I suppose it's no surprise that the idea of investigating the commune culture has hit more than one of us at the same time. The phenomenon has been mushrooming and I can find practically nothing at all about it in the data banks."

Fry said, disgruntled, "I just hope nobody has come up with my subject. I'll never get my doctorate if I do no more than duplicate somebody else's thesis."

Ted said, changing the subject, "What in the world were you doing out on the road this time of morning?"

The other chuckled in self-deprecation. "I drove all the way through from Denver and just arrived. I'm probably the only funker in the country still afraid of aircraft."

The steak had arrived and Ted Swain tore into it. Gerald Fry poured more coffee.

Halfway through the meat and potato, Ted Swain became so tired he couldn't finish. "I'm going to have to go to bed," he said. "I don't know how to thank you."

"Nothing," Fry said. "But you still might not be completely out of the woods. I'll stay on for a few hours and watch your TV. Then, when it's a little later, I'll drive on over to Jissom. I've checked out quite a few of the drug-culture communes in the West but

139

possibly there are some regional differences. For instance, down in the Southwest they use a lot of peyote, but it's unknown farther north."

"Peyote?"

"Mescaline. It's a hallucinogen but not nearly as strong as LSD-25. Comes from a form of cactus."

"I've got to get to bed," Ted said. "Thanks again."

"Possibly I'll drop in again after seeing Jissom. We could compare notes."

"Wizard," Ted told him, making his way from the kitchen to the living room and beyond to his bedroom.

On the way, something, he didn't know what, made him look into his study. He didn't even have to enter to note that, once again, his desk had been ransacked.

He shook his head. He wasn't up to investigating now. He went over to his bed and flaked out, not bothering to get out of his clothes. He was asleep while his head was still two or three inches from the pillow.

Chapter Fifteen

Ted Swain was awakened by his TV phone.

He ran an unhappy hand over his face and activated the bedside instrument. It was Henry Neville, his ferret face irritated.

He said, "Are you in bed this time of day, Swain?"

Ted shot a look at the window. It was obviously well into the afternoon. He said, "I was up all night. Just a minute, I'll take this on my screen in my study."

He got up and went into the bathroom and stared for a moment into the mirror. His face was a mess. He vaguely remembered rubbing the mucus from his nose all over it. And he remembered rolling on the floor, there at Jissom, grinding his face into the heavy rug. He threw cold water onto it, and, drying it, went through the living room and into the study. He tossed the towel onto a chair, took his place at the desk and switched on the phone.

The National Security official was looking impatient. He said, "Look here, Doctor Swain, I have a suggestion about your researches on the communes. Not far from where you live is one that particularly calls for looking into. It's near the town of Bearsville and . . ."

"Jissom," Ted said wearily.

"How did you know? From what meager reports I

have, it is evidently rife with narcotics, some of them illegal, and undoubtedly criminal elements are among their number."

Ted said, pulling one of his large ears, "That's where I was last night. They slipped me an LSD mickey and I was under its influence for something like ten or twelve hours. I've just pulled out of it."

"You mean to tell me they gave you an illegal drug without your permission! Why?"

Ted Swain took a deep breath. "Mr. Neville, somehow or other they knew my reports would get to you and Dollar. They'd been tipped off. They put me on the LSD so they could question me thoroughly. I have no doubt that I spilled everything I knew, including the fact that you suspect the communes to be full of subversives."

"You fool!" the other snapped.

Ted Swain sighed. "Everybody's a fool under LSD. I didn't take it because I wanted to. At any rate, they already knew I was cooperating with you and Academician Dollar. That might be something for you to look into. Where's the leak?"

"Who gave you the LSD and submitted you to questioning? That's an illegal act."

"They called themselves John, Clark and Jimmy, and I suspect all three names were phony. I have no way of proving they did it. There were no other witnesses. I suspect that on the approach of your men, they'd disappear. You'd certainly not get any cooperation from the rest of the commune. I've got a disk recording of the early part of our session, but they broke my portable bug before giving me the LSD. All three of their voices are on the recording, but I have no evidence that I was under LSD. It's worn off now."

The other's irritation grew. "Have you made any reports as yet on the communes you've thus far seen?"

"Not yet. I'll be working on it today."

"Have you run into anything of the nature of what we discussed in the academician's escape room?"

"Not really. Oh, one thing. My study, here in my

home, has twice been ransacked since I began this research."

"Searched? Why? Is anything missing? Didn't the identity screen on your door record anyone who entered? You could check with the data banks. They would have a record."

"I tried that the first time. No record of anyone entering the house. Nothing is missing. I can't imagine what anyone was looking for."

"It sounds ridiculous to me. Do you want me to send a man over?"

"I don't see what he could find. As I say, nothing is missing, so far as I know."

The older man shook his head. "Well, carry on, Swain. Be sure you get names if you run into any of the evidence I'm looking for."

"Yes sir," Ted Swain said. The face faded.

He looked at the empty screen for a spell. Henry Neville was irritated by Ted's experience in Jissom and he couldn't afford to irritate the National Security Forces higher-up. The other was too close to Englebrecht. However, there had been no manner of avoiding his Jissom session. There was nothing he could do about it.

He checked out his desk but had been correct in what he'd reported to Neville. Nothing had been taken. Some of the papers he had made notes upon the day before were moved around a bit, that was all. If it hadn't been for his quirk of memory, recalling the exact position in which he'd left things, he would never have known his study had been entered.

He checked with the data banks again and got the answer he expected. There was no record, from the identity screens on his doors, of anyone entering the house. Since the screens were functioning, entry should have been impossible.

He gave it up.

Ted went into the kitchen-dining room, just to check on whether or not the redhead, Gerald Fry, had left. And, of course, he had. He had liked the other, who

143

had so freely gone out of his way to assist a complete stranger, and rather hoped that he would return to compare notes. It would be interesting to see how he made out in Jissom. At least it was unlikely that he'd allow them to give him the LSD treatment they'd given to Ted Swain.

He went back to the bathroom, suddenly feeling the accumulated filth of the past twenty-four hours. He stripped and threw all of his clothing, even the kilt, into the disposal chute. He showered long and with care. When he at long last felt completely clean, he wrapped a towel about his waist and went back into the kitchen-dining room and to his order box there.

He dialed West Hurley's ultramarket and ordered a complete new outfit. The day looked excellent, a leftover of summer, so he selected a sports shirt, walking shorts, high wool socks and hiking shoes. He waited impatiently for several minutes and, when the tiny red light on the order box glowed, he opened it and took out the clothing.

Ted returned with it to the bedroom, dressed and then went on into his study.

He wasn't particularly a news-hound, but he hadn't found the time in the past few days to listen at all, so he dialed for a three-day highlights of world developments on his TV library-booster screen and settled back to listen and watch.

A new discovery in Common Europe improved the cancer treatment now being utilized.

Also in the medical world the last known case of syphilis in United America had been located and cured.

Another baby had been born in the Reunited Nations moon colony. How many was that now? Three or four. Ted Swain couldn't help but feel sorry for the kids. They were being used as guinea pigs and undoubtedly, what with the gravity in which they'd been born and would spend the early years of their lives, they would never be able to come to the mother planet, earth. Earth gravity would immobilize them. It was bad enough on those moon colonists who remained for as long as a year.

Warren Edgar, the Chief Director of the National Security Forces had gotten his 50,000 extra men. They would be computer selected on next muster day. A small army. Ted Swain wondered, all over again, what in the name of the holy Zoroaster Edgar thought he needed them for. Would any of them be assigned to Henry Neville's region? He assumed so. They'd be ass-deep in security agents.

China was embarking on the irrigation of the Gobi desert, utilizing ocean water, desalted by fusion power and then pumped the couple of thousand miles through pipes. Well, that'd keep them busy for a generation or so. He wondered how the reforestation of the Sahara was coming along. That was an even bigger project. He understood that they could now grow trees as fast as they could flowers.

The news over, he went on back to his commune notes and his reports for Englebrecht, and spent the balance of the afternoon on them. The material, admittedly, was accumulating. But one thing became clear to him. He wasn't staying long enough in any of the communes. He had insufficient data upon how they governed themselves, for instance. What he was going to have to do was remain for several days in a row in the places he visited, interview commune officials in more depth, that sort of thing.

Which reminded him. He dialed the ultramarket and ordered another electronic bug to replace the one John had destroyed in Jissom. Which reminded him all over again. How had John known that Ted Swain was cooperating with Neville and Dollar? He worried the question awhile and then had to shrug it off as unanswerable.

He wrapped it up finally and dialed Academician Englebrecht's apartment in University City V11. His director of dissertation wasn't in and the call was taken by Brian Fitz, his limp-wristed secretary.

Ted said, "I've got some reports here that the academician wanted. I'll put them on the screen for you to duplicate."

"Very good, Doctor Swain."

Ted Swain put the pages he had voco-typed on the screen one by one and, when he had finished, said, "It might be a good idea to make three copies of each, Fitz. Henry Neville and George Dollar also wanted copies."

"Very well," the other said primly.

Something came to Ted and he said, "By the way, do you know of a commune called, let's see, New Tangier?"

The other simpered, there could be no different word for it. "Oh, yes. There are ever so many wonderful chaps who live there. I didn't know you were interested."

Ted cleared his throat. "How about Gomorrah?"

"Oh, now really. You mustn't go there ... Ted. They're really too much for a nice boy. Oh, truly."

Ted said, "Thanks for the warning. So long, Fitz."

"Bye-bye, but do call me Brian . . . Teddy."

Ted Swain flicked off. Zo-ro-as-ter. From now on he was going to have to be careful about being alone with Brian Fitz. As he had long suspected, Englebrecht's personal secretary was as queer as chicken shit, as Gloria, at Lesbos, had put it.

The identity screen on his front door buzzed and he activated his desk screen to check. His eyes widened. It was Sue Benny Voss, the girl artist from New Woodstock. That brought something back too. During his LSD hallucinations he had been torn with need for her. Why Sue Benny Voss? During the past few days he had also been utilized as a stud by such superlative specimens as Terpsichore, Bethie McBride and—what was her name?—Marsha.

He flicked the door switch, came to his feet and went into the living room to welcome his visitor. How had she known where he lived? Possibly he had told her. Or, for that matter, she could have checked through the data banks. He had informed her that he attended the university city.

The door opened and she entered his living room. She seemed very young and vulnerable in the heavy frame of the doorway, with her blond hair piled up on her head, and her throat as fragile as a child's, ivory-white except for a faint blue vein pulsing against the smooth skin. She wore slim black slacks and a white sweater with a high cowl that framed her head and made her face look small and pale and innocent. Her appearance was a far cry from what it had been in New Woodstock.

"Sue Benny," he said happily, advancing to greet her. Away from her own surroundings, out of her artistic element, she was a different woman—not that he hadn't liked the original. There was a hesitant something about her, a worriedness.

"Sit down," he told her. "Let me get you a drink."

She rubbed her arms with her hands and shook her head. She said, "Did you tell about me in your report to the police?"

He came to a halt and stared at her. "Report to the police? That's not the way I'd put it."

"How would you put it?" she said bitterly.

"I told you the truth. I'm working on a dissertation for my academician's degree. It will be about ancient and modern communes. My progress reports go to my director of dissertation. It's only a side issue, a coincidence, that George Dollar, the local head of the National Data Banks, and Henry Neville, the director of the regional National Security Forces, are interested in the material I collect."

She looked at him intently, evidently deciding that he was telling the truth as he saw it.

She began pacing, with her hands locked around her elbows and an intense little frown gathering between her eyes. The soles of her shoes made a whispering sound on the thick carpeting and the muscles of her smooth calves flexed to the rhythm of her restless footsteps.

147

"Then you did mention me in your reports?"

He stared at her, upset. "I . . . I'm afraid I did, Sue Benny. It never occurred to me not to. I thought you were the most interesting single item I ran into in New Woodstock. A really typical member of a commune."

She stopped and faced him. "But don't you see? I'm an alien. Although I'm not eligible for it myself, in actuality I'm living on Universal Guaranteed Income. I could be arrested for defrauding the government."

He sank down into a chair, distressed. "It simply never occurred to me."

"You told all about the workings of New Woodstock? How we pooled our resources and those not eligible for UGI took from the common community fund?"

He nodded, dumbly.

She said, "At least the others are American citizens. I'm not. Has Director Neville already got that report?"

"By this time, yes."

"Then I'm on the run, Ted."

"What . . . what can I do? Anything in my power, Sue Benny." His heart seemed to do a leisurely somersault within his rib cage. She was the last person he would have wanted to harm. And she had been so secure, so adjusted, there in the mobile art colony.

She sat down across from him. "I discussed it with Bat Hardin. They're speeding up the gathering of the mobile homes that will make up the commune. They're going to take off for Mexico within a week. I'll cross the border and join them there. Meanwhile, I have to hide."

"Right here, of course."

She nodded at that, as though it were what she had expected him to say. "And I'll need some way of getting to Mexico."

"I'll drive you down, when the time comes." He considered it. "Even if they do look for you—and I wouldn't put it beyond Neville, in view of the fact that he's so hot against the communes. But they wouldn't dream of looking here."

He dug into his pocket, came up with his transceiver and flicked the time button. He checked the hour and said, "Are you hungry? I'm beginning to realize I'm famished. We can go on over to the community restaurant."

"Wizard," she said, standing again. "From now on, you have a full-time sponger on your hands."

"I can hack it, particularly in view of the fact that it's my fault. How did you know I'd made those reports?"

They started for the door which, as always, opened automatically at their approach.

She frowned and said, "Bat Hardin told me about it. Where he learned, I don't know."

It was the same thing as had happened at Jissom. Somehow, they had discovered that Ted's reports were going to Neville and Dollar.

They started down the street toward the community buildings, Ted taking her arm. He said, "I'll go over tomorrow and apologize to Hardin."

"You'd better not," she said, looking at him obliquely.

"Well, why? This calls for an apology."

"Some of the men are on the bitter side. You've really roached them. There might be a bad scene."

"I see," he said, then maintained silence during the rest of their walk to the restaurant. He had it coming to him, he supposed.

He couldn't figure out how he was going to handle such things in the future. The support of Neville and Dollar in this project was priceless to him. On the other hand, he didn't like the role of informer, especially when it involved such persons as Sue Benny Voss. The fact was, she was illegal. Through a fluke during her childhood, she had never become a citizen. As a result of that, she was currently, by the laws of United America, a criminal if she subsisted on UGI. Theoretically, it was his duty to report her. Theoretically.

In actuality, the amount she consumed illegally was

a drop in the ocean of the country's abundance. It was meaningless.

The community restaurant with its modern decor, its subdued lighting, made an instant hit with Sue Benny. "You know, this is one of the things we miss in a mobile town. It would be possible, but not really practical, for us to have a small mobile restaurant. In truth, we all usually eat in our own homes."

"So do I, usually," Ted said, leading her toward the bar. "You can either dial a meal from the community kitchens, cook your own, or come here to eat. I'm a cook-your-own type."

"Hmmm," she said. "You look more like a rail splitter than a chef, Honest Abe."

"Don't roach me," he said. Then, to an occupant of one of the bar stools, "What spins, Mike?"

Mike Latimer turned from his drink and took them in. "Hello, Ted. How did a nice girl, as this obviously is, ever wind up with you?"

Ted said, "Sue Benny Voss, I hate to have to introduce you, but this is Mike Latimer, West Hurley's gift to the airwaves."

They shook hands. Mike frowned and said, "Sue Benny, Sue Benny." He snapped his fingers. "Ted's girl in the Mobile Art Commune."

Chapter Sixteen

The two of them looked aghast at the news commentator, then at each other.

"What's spinning with you?" Mike said. "Have a drink on me?" He looked at Sue Benny. "How about Margaritas, to celebrate your trip down to Mexico? That's where your mobile art commune is going, isn't it? Latin America? I was over to New Woodstock just the other day to pick up an item. Sounds like quite a jazzer of a project to me."

Sue Benny looked weakly at Ted.

There was nothing for it. Ted said to Mike Latimer, "Look, Mike, in view of your great love and admiration for Henry Neville, I'm going to lay things on the table. If you work some little item of gossip into your next broadcast, some of your typical drivel, such as 'Man about town Ted Swain is being seen these days with artist Sue Benny Voss, from the mobile art commune of New Woodstock,' she's sunk."

"Sunk?"

"Sunk. She's on the lam from Neville's National Security Forces. The charge is a minor one but he's so goosed off about the communes that he'd bust one of their members for spitting in a gutter."

Mike looked from Sue Benny to Ted and back. "I don't get it."

Ted said, "Sue Benny isn't a citizen. It's illegal for her to be living off Universal Guaranteed Income, which she does, indirectly, in the commune."

"Oh," Mike said. "Well, what's the big problem? I'm mum."

She thanked him with a small smile.

"I don't believe I've ever had a Margarita," she said.

They had Margaritas. They had another round of Margaritas. Then they went over to a table and studied the menu. Ted Swain realized how out of whack his eating schedule had become. He'd had half a whale steak and a potato at dawn of this day and nothing since.

They ordered and Sue Benny said, "Either of you hombres have a cigarette?"

Mike said, "Tobacco or pot?" reaching for a pocket.

She said, "I never smoke tobacco. It's bad for you."

"Ummm." He offered a cigarette and lit it for her, then looked at Ted. "How's the investigation into the communes going? Been knocked over the head yet?"

"Almost," Ted told him. "Last night I went over to Jissom and they fed me some LSD in a drink. I compressed a lost weekend into twelve hours. It seemed they'd been tipped off that copies of my reports were to go to Neville and Dollar and wanted to know the details. I didn't have any details they already didn't know. That's all there is to it. I still feel fagged from it."

"Some of those kids in Jissom are tough characters," Mike nodded. "You're lucky they didn't kick your face in, snooping around like that. Why don't you give the whole project up?"

"I'm beginning to wonder," Ted said, his voice sour. "But it's my big chance."

"Where do you go next?"

Ted Swain thought about it. "Walden, I suppose. That agricultural commune you mentioned up in the area they used to call Vermont. Thus far I haven't run into any settlements where they actually produce their own food. They make wine at New Athens but the other communes evidently depend entirely on Universal Guaranteed Income and the pay of the commune members who work."

"An agricultural commune," Sue Benny said. "That sounds interesting. I've heard that there's quite a few of them throughout the country. Sort of a back-to-the-soil razzle."

"Well, watch your step," Mike said.

After they'd finished dinner they said their goodbyes to Mike Latimer and strolled back to the house.

The moonlight was filtering through a light gray fog but they could see the massive bulk of the mountains against the sky, and slender trees twisting in a wind that had come up. Ted Swain was surprisingly tired. His legs ached with each step and he had to breathe deeply to get enough air into his lungs. But his body seemed separate from him, as if it were some large and clumsily wrapped package which he had been carrying for too long a distance. He wondered how long he had to wait to be completely free of his bout with the LSD.

They had remained quiet during the walk but when they entered the living room of the house she turned to him, enabling Ted to look at her and admire the play of humor and intelligence in her face and eyes.

He said, "There's only one bed, I'm afraid."

She laughed softly. "Wizard, and there's only two of us. I assume it's a double. Or were you going to play it noble and sleep on the couch?"

"The bedroom's in here," he said. "If you don't mind, we'll hit the hay. I'm still roached by that bad trip I took in Jissom."

They went into the bedroom and undressed, seated on opposite sides of the king-size bed. Since she had no nightgown he too remained nude.

Living in a mobile home had robbed Sue Benny of furniture of this magnitude. She said, "Why, you could lose a girl in a bed like this."

"Never fear," he told her. "Sue Benny. Where in the

153

holy name of Zoroaster did you get a moniker like that? It doesn't sound like Common Europe."

.She said, "My father was an admirer of Eugene Sue, who wrote *The Wandering Jew*. He also had a friend named Benjamin. Since you could hardly call a girl 'Benjamin,' he shortened it to Benny."

Ted Swain slid into the bed and said in exhaustion, "In spite of you naming me Paul Bunyun the other morning, I'm afraid I'm in no shape to perform."

"You're forgiven. Good night, darling."

But he was already asleep.

In the morning it was different, and Ted Swain rediscovered why it had been Sue Benny who had come to him in his LSD hallucinations. The girl was completely frank, completely liberated from any sexual restraints. She was willing and laughingly eager to practice any variations he could come up with and he maneuvered her about into half a dozen positions, bringing her to climax over and over again before giving her the full benefit of his male juices.

She murmured finally, deliciously, "Why do people ever get out of bed?"

He laughed. "I don't know about women, but after a time a man begins to feel like a dishrag."

For a long time they lay there. There was a sense of drowsy, comfortable communion between them and they talked in a rambling fashion, with little real interest, about other times, other places, other people. She told him of her earlier life; he, his.

They both decided that they had never been in love before, not really. There had been a good deal of sex for both, but only sex.

He said finally, "I'll be going up to Walden today."

"Then you're going to continue with this commune investigation?"

He hesitated, but only momentarily. "Yes. Yes, I'm going to have to. I plan to stay there several days, this time. I want to really get the feel of a commune, not just a surface impression. That is, I'll stay if they have any facilities for strangers. Why don't you come along?

Without a transceiver of your own, you wouldn't be able to order anything you needed. I could leave you a supply of food, of course, but if anything else came up you'd have to do without."

"I . . . haven't any clothes, or things. I left everything in the trailer."

"You'd better not return to New Woodstock for them. They might be looking for you. Later on we'll get in touch with Bat Hardin and make arrangements for him to drive your trailer down to Mexico. But now we'll order what you need from the West Hurley ultramarket. I've got suitcases."

They bathed and dressed leisurely and then went into the dining room and ordered large breakfasts.

She smiled at him over the table and said, "Old married pair."

Ted Swain looked at her and noticed the hollows under her eyes, soft and dark against her white skin. She was more than pretty, more than just beautiful, she was unbelievably handsome. All aside from her intelligence, humor and charm.

He said, "Do you want to be married?"

She thought about it. "I don't see any reason. Why does anyone bother to be married anymore? All children are legitimate, assuming you want children, and I don't. Not at this point in my life, at least. I'm all in favor of the birth rate staying at its present zero growth."

He said, "I assume that if I were married to you there would be some manner in which I could devote part of my Universal Guaranteed Income to your support. Possibly even, you could become a citizen. I could find out. I'm not really up on such things."

"It would involve my not taking the trip to Latin America."

"Yes, it would involve that."

"I'm an artist," she said in a soft, breaking voice. She closed her eyes and ran both hands over her thick blond hair, pulling it tightly back from her forehead in

155

a gesture of distress. "Places like New Woodstock are my habitat, darling."

He didn't answer that. She said softly, "I'll think about it."

They pushed the remainder of their breakfasts back to the center of the table and let it sink away, then went to the order box to dial for her requirements from the community ultramarket. Womanlike, she took her time at the screen, examining what seemed, to an impatient Ted Swain, an endless multitude of products.

He went on into the bedroom, brought forth two suitcases, and did his own packing. He planned on remaining for at least three days in Walden, but if his supply of clothing ran short he could buy more from local ultramarkets.

Finally, Sue Benny entered with her new things and they finished the packing and on his transceiver he summoned an electrosteamer. He gave the usual instructions to his TV phone and to the door identity screen and they went on out to the curb before his house and waited for the vehicle which shortly came smoothing up.

"Surface or underground?" he asked her, taking the seat behind the manual controls as she slid in beside him.

"Oh, surface. I never go underground if I can help it."

"Wizard," he said. "Sage. I feel the same way. Look up the coordinates for Walden, will you? I assume the town is marked on the map."

She fished in the dash compartment, got the map and found the required information. He dialed and settled back as the car took off.

More than half of the trip was a delight, at this time of the year. They took their time, stopping leisurely for lunch and dinner at wayside automated restaurants. Later it began clouding up and the countryside became less charming.

It began to drizzle and then rain as they came into the Walden area, to the east of Lake Bomoseen. Long rumblings of thunder sounded off to their right and lightning split the darkness about them. Omen, Ted Swain thought glumly, nice cheery omens. The windshield ran with water and the wipers slapped it vigorously from side to side, but visibility was cut down to the few yards which their headlights were able to bore through the spuming rain. It was bleak, inhospitable country they drove through; skimpy oaks and maples, their trunks crusted with rank growths of thorn brush, flung their branches about in the noisy winds. Occasionally, light could be seen through mists rising from the sodden ground, but the area seemed largely deserted, with rain-black trees and marshes stretching off to the darkness of either side of the electrosteamer. Houses began to loom ahead of them against a backdrop of night-dark skies and flying clouds.

"If this is Walden, it looks like a bad scene to me," Ted growled to his companion.

"Rain and night don't help," Sue Benny said. "It's Walden, all right. I saw a sign back there."

"The houses are all spread out," he muttered, putting the car on manual control and taking over. "But I suppose that would apply in a farming community. The whole place looks like one of those old historical movies set at about the time of the Civil War."

"They're obviously carrying on the traditions of this area. That's a beautiful barn, over there. I'd like to at least sketch it, if we can stay."

"If this is like the other communes, there'll be some sort of town hall, or other administration buildings. But there doesn't seem to be. This place stretches all over hell and beyond. We'd have our work cut out finding it."

"Why not stop at one of the houses and ask directions?"

"Wizard. There's one near the road."

He drove up to the porch, as near as he could get. "You stay here. I'll get the scenario."

He opened the door and made a dash for it. The

157

path up to the porch was muddy and his shoes were heavy with it by the time he got to shelter.

The house was made of wood and the lighted windows were curtained. He sought in vain for an identity screen or even a bell, and finally knocked.

A voice, resonant and deep, told him to come in.

Chapter Seventeen

Ted did, after wiping his feet as thoroughly as he could on the welcome mat.

He entered a living room that was an anachronism. Seemingly all had been designed to reproduce the farm house of the early 20th Century. It was warm enough, heated by an iron pot-belly stove, comfortable enough, in the old tradition. On the floor were rag rugs, obviously handmade. So was the furniture, sturdy, without nonsense, without finish save wax. A table, two cabinets, a sideboard, half a dozen straight chairs, a couch with various homemade pillows in dark colors, two rocking chairs. On the walls were framed samplers declaring that *Jesus Never Fails* and similar sentiments.

One of the rocking chairs was occupied by a woman plying knitting needles. There were wrinkles in her face, not too many and not too deep, and her hair, a good honest shade of gray, was drawn tightly back into a roll at the nape of her neck. With all this, her eyes were youthful and sharp and there was a strength in the sharp thrust of her chin and the high-arched lines of her rather prominent nose. She radiated an aura of age-old motherhood.

The room's other occupant stood before the second rocking chair. He held a black book in his right hand, undoubtedly a bible. He was tall and middle-aged but with only a scattering of gray in his hair, and flecks of silver in his bold mustache. He wore a dark suit which looked like tweed, so thick and stiff and rough that Ted wondered how he stood it. But the other didn't look the sort to heed protests of flesh—from himself or anyone else. His face was like a crag or rock, hewn into its present contours by freezing winds and waves, and his appearance was as majestic as a clipper flying under full sail.

He looked at Ted Swain inquiringly but said, "Welcome to the hospitality of my home. You are a fugitive from the elements?"

Ted said, "Not exactly. I'm looking for the commune of Walden."

"We do not call ourselves a commune, outlander, but this is Walden. I am Wilhelm Langenscheidt and this is my good wife Emma."

"My name is Theodore Swain," Ted said, advancing to shake a work-gnarled brown hand. "We had a little trouble getting located, the rain's so bad."

"We?" the farmer said.

"My . . . wife is out in the car."

"You must bring the poor thing in," the woman said, putting down her needles. "I'll make a pot of coffee." She stood, then proceeded to leave through a door at the other end of the living room. Her dress was dark, colorless, and extended to her ankles.

Ted said, "Actually, we were looking for the administration center, or whatever you call it. If Walden has accommodations, we wished to spend at least two or three nights."

"The town hall would be closed at this time of night," the big man said. "Nor do we have accommodations for outlanders. What is that which you seek?"

Ted said cautiously, "We're looking into the various communes. I have heard about Walden and wanted to find out about it. How you operate, how you cooperate, how you govern your community. That sort of thing."

"We have no inn, no hotel, but you are free to stay

160

with us. Since the children have grown ..." his face grew stern here " ... and have seen fit to go out into the crass world to seek ways other than those of Walden, Mother and I live alone."

"Why ... we couldn't impose on you."

"It is the right of the traveler to expect hospitality, and the duty of the homeowner to extend it. And if you seek information of Walden, this is a worthy house for you to base yourself in. I am one of the elders this year."

Elder? That must be something like the town-council members of other communes. Ted felt that he had hit the jackpot. He came to a sudden decision.

"I'll go get my wife and our luggage. I still feel it's an imposition, but you're very kind."

Langenscheidt followed him to the door and the two of them hurried to the car.

Ted shouted to Sue Benny, "Into the house!" as he wrestled open the back door and got out their two bags. The big farmer took one of them, and all three dashed back to the shelter of the porch, Sue Benny holding her hands over her head in a futile effort to ward off some of the rain.

Ted said, "We were drivel-happy not to bring raincoats and umbrellas but the day was so pleasant earlier."

Their host opened the door and led the way in, putting the suitcase down near the bottom of a staircase leading to the second floor.

Ted put his bag down as well and said, "Sue Benny, this is Mr. Langenscheidt."

Sue Benny smiled her warmth and extended a hand but Langenscheidt said, his voice heavy, "Please do not call me 'mister.' The term is derived from 'master' and I do not desire to be anyone's master, no more than I desire to be mastered. It is a term for slaves, not free men."

"Sorry," Ted said mildly.

The other gave Sue Benny's hand a quick one-two shake, then dropped it and gestured to chairs. "Please

161

rest yourselves. Mother will be here shortly with coffee and kuchen. You have eaten your supper?"

Ted said, "We stopped at an autocafeteria on the way."

The other shook his head. "Such food is an abomination."

Sue Benny, even as she sank into a chair, in relief, said, "What's wrong with it?"

The farmer resumed his rocking chair. He said, "It is no longer of the soil. It is of the machine. The fields are ultramated, the so-called farmer often living and doing his work a hundred miles or more from the fields which he works with remote-control machinery. The flour mills are ultramated to the point where only one or two men are needed to supervise. The bakeries are the same. The bread produced is untouched by human hands from the time the wheat is planted until the time it is put into the mouth of the consumer. The same applies to practically all other foods."

Ted Swain had taken a chair too. Their hostess entered, bearing a wooden tray complete with coffee pot, milk, sugar, and what looked like gingerbread. Ted hadn't eaten gingerbread since he'd been a child.

Service was gently gracious. Sue Benny was served, Ted was served and then Langenscheidt filled his own heavy mug with coffee. He took it black and unsweetened, the way he obviously took life.

He said, "And what is it you seek to learn in Walden, Brother?"

Ted sipped his coffee experimentally. He considered himself a coffee buff and insisted on a particular blend that came from Columbia. With this dark brew he could have closed his eyes in pain. Only a sadist would have produced it, he felt unhappily, as he looked at the gentle soul who had served them; and only a masochist would drink it.

Ted said to his host, "Well, sir . . ."

"Please do not call me 'sir.' The word is derived from 'sire,' a feudalistic term meaning 'lord.' I do not wish to be someone else's lord any more than I wish someone else to lord it over me. I am a free man."

Ted took a deep breath. "Sorry. But I am studying the communes. I am to write a book about them. Throughout the nation millions of persons are dropping out of what our officials would like to think is the norm. They're gathering in communes, leaving the pseudocities with their hi-rise multi-thousanded mini-apartments and moving to communities of varying sizes with a common theme. They largely subsist on their Universal Guaranteed Income and . . ."

"Not all do." The heavy-set farmer was definite.

"I beg your pardon?"

"We of Walden do not live on charity. We live by our own toil."

Ted Swain looked his surprise. He said, un-believingly, "You mean none of you utilize your UGI?"

"None of us. Each quarter it is issued to us but none accept, Brother."

Sue Benny looked from Langenscheidt to his wife and back, mystified. "But how do you rent your elec-trosteamers, your, well, tractors and farm things such as that? I don't know much about farming."

"We don't. We have horses and wagons, and raise and make our own. Man was fated by God to live by the sweat of his brow. That is the holy word." He looked at Ted severely. "Do you read the Good Book?"

"I got as far as the begats."

"Do you jest with me? All too few read the bible in this age."

"It went out of fashion, when thinking came in. But wait a moment. There are some things you simply can't make by yourself. By what I see, you've probably built this house yourself, you, and, I imagine, your friends, and you've even made the furnishings. And un-doubtedly you grow your own food and make your own clothing. But there are some things you can't make, that you have to use credits for. Medicine, postage, phone calls, and things that simply can't be

163

produced in this part of the world. This coffee, for instance, and there's no steel here. How do you make plows? There's no salt. How do you get salt?"

The older man held up a brown hand to stem the tide. "We produce various handicrafts when we are not at work in the fields. Some of the outlanders value them, there is so little left in this world of ours that is handmade. We trade our surpluses of them for the things you mention. Suppose, for instance, that Mother makes a quilt and that I need iron for the blacksmith so that I can have made a harrow. Someone who wishes the quilt uses his Universal Guaranteed Income credit to secure the iron for me."

Ted Swain was ogling him once more. "Then you've gone back to what amounts to primitive barter?"

The other nodded. "If that is what you wish to call it."

Sue Benny said, "But why? If you collected your UGI you could live in comfort without your heavy farm work. You'd have a life of leisure."

The big farmer looked at her levelly. "Man was not meant to possess unlimited leisure time, Sister. Give it to him and he can fall apart. Down through the ages he worked, and he worked twelve or more hours a day. Every day. Or he starved. What to do with his time was determined for him. What recreation there was, was very seldom; purely traditional games and dances were a vast relief and entertainment. He never got a chance to become bored with them; he got to play them too seldom. That situation lasted for 99.99 percent of the history of the species."

"But now we have beaten nature," Ted Swain said. "Now we don't have to work like that. We have time to devote to the arts and sciences, to becoming scholars and developing ourselves."

Langenscheidt turned his eyes back to Ted. His wife had resumed her practiced knitting, and placidly rocked in her chair.

"But most of mankind is not creative, nor inclined to the scholarly life. To kill time—and killing time is not

164

murder but suicide, Theodore Swain—he resorts to ever more frivolous entertainment, to the misuse of alcohol and even narcotics. Sex becomes meaningless, as an act of true love, because it is so available. The whole world becomes promiscuous. The family as we knew it disappears. It is not a happy life, Theodore Swain. These people of one-hundred-percent leisure are a frustrated people. Rome, with its free bread and circuses, is a frightening example of a nation which no longer has to work."

"The Romans never bothered to educate their proletariat to the proper use of leisure," Ted said musingly. "It might take us a generation or so, but we should be able to raise our people to participate in the arts and sciences rather than simply pursuing shallow entertainment. Perhaps the communes are a step in that direction. But, at any rate, here in Walden you've gone back to the old ways, eh?"

"Yes. And here in Walden we find happiness in a life of toil. Here, Robert Owen lives."

Without looking up from her work, though her thin colorless lips moved a little in an impersonal smile, Emma Langenscheidt entered the conversation for the first time. She said, "Yes, in Walden, Robert Owen lives."

And suddenly a half dozen pieces began to fall into place in the puzzles that had been confusing Doctor Theodore Swain.

He said to Sue Benny, "I've changed my mind. We won't stay. We're going back to West Hurley tonight."

She bug-eyed him as though he had suddenly become demented. "But, Walden. How about your investigation of Walden?"

He said slowly, "It won't be necessary now." His face went bitterly wry. "It never was."

Ted came to his feet and looked at his host and hostess, who were also staring at him. He said, "Thanks for your hospitality and your offer to put us up. However, something has suddenly come to me and I have to get back to take care of it."

He turned and headed for the door, taking up the suitcases on the way and Sue Benny followed him hurriedly, saying over her shoulder, "Thank you very much. I haven't the slightest idea what's spinning with him."

Wilhelm Langenscheidt came after them and stood in the doorway to call, "Though you are not a believer, go with the Lord," as they dashed through the rain for the car.

Ted held the door open for her, tossed the bags into the back, then hurried around to his own side.

Ted Swain dialed the coordinates of West Hurley, choosing the underground expressway. He didn't know where the nearest entry was, with its dispatch coordinator, but the automated vehicle could worry about that. Doing it underground would speed up the trip considerably. The car took off and he settled back in his seat, his mouth working.

Sue Benny said, "I simply don't get the scenario. What happened all of a sudden? What spins?"

"I'm not clear yet. I've got to think it out and to clear up some loose ends. This project of mine has just fallen apart."

She could see that he was in no frame of mind to discuss it and lapsed into her own silence. This hombre was turning out to be a real jazzer.

After a time, she said, "You wouldn't know a Gerald Fry, would you?"

He turned to look his surprise at her. "Gerald Fry!"

"Yes. It seems that he was doing research similar to yours. That is, he was looking into the communes."

"How did you know about him?"

"While you were in the house there, at first, I turned on the TV screen for the news. He's dead. He was killed in an accident."

"Accident!"

"It seems to be quite a mystery. His electrosteamer was forced off the road, some way or other, and crashed into a stone fence. It seems impossible, unless both vehicles were under manual control. Who ever hears of car accidents anymore? At any rate, the commentator said that he was investigating the communes."

He sank back into his seat, appalled. He muttered, "Yes, who ever hears of car accidents anymore?"

He murmured, "We can make it by the midnight broadcast."

He redialed for a new destination.

"Where are we going?" she said.

"Kingston. To the broadcasting station."

She leaned back, giving it all up.

When they emerged from the underground expressway, Ted Swain took over manually and headed for the TV station, which was located on the outskirts of town. Kingston was only a few miles from West Hurley and was the largest pseudocity in the vicinity, boasting half a dozen hi-rise ultraapartment houses, as well as older buildings. It was losing its population, Ted Swain knew. The trend in living was to smaller towns, and away from the pseudocities.

It was no longer raining. Ted parked before the rather small building, which was set into a small park. He had been there but once before, when he had picked up Mike Latimer for a luncheon date. There were comparatively few local programs, so there was no need for a larger establishment for this area. Mike had an office where he assembled his material. The place was so automated that sometimes he was alone save for one technician.

When Ted and Sue Benny entered the visitors' room, Mike Latimer was on lens. They could see him through the large plate window, sitting at a desk. A small red light, above a clock, was lit, indicating that the studio was hot. To one side of Mike, a lone technician sat, yawning, in a control booth.

Mike Latimer obviously saw them enter but, being on lens, couldn't make any gesture of greeting, though he must have been surprised by their presence.

Ted and Sue Benny took chairs and waited. It was the first time that she had ever been in a broadcasting

167

station and was interested; though there was precious little to see.

Mike was saying, " . . . and that's the news, folks. This is station WAN, the Voice and Eyes of the Hudson Valley, coming to you from Kingston. And this is Michael Latimer, the town crier, the regional gossip, signing off until tomorrow at noon." He cued the engineer by saying, "Let's get back to the network, Johnny."

The red light flickered off, indicating that the studio was no longer hot, and Mike waved to them with one hand, rubbing the back of his neck with his other. Ted Swain knew that he tensed up, on lens.

The news commentator came over to the heavy studio door and entered the room in which they sat.

"Surprise, surprise," he said. "What in the name of holy jumping Zoroaster are you two doing out of bed this time of night?"

Ted came to his feet and looked into the other's eyes. "Robert Owen lives," he said.

Chapter Eighteen

Mike Latimer looked at him for a long, empty moment, then his natural smile came to his lips. "And will never die," he said. "Then, you've become one of us?"

"Not exactly," Ted said. "So that's the answer to your password."

"How'd you find out, if you haven't been recruited? Frankly, I didn't think you were membership material."

"I guessed. I've been hearing it too often these past few days for it to be coincidence. You've got some sort of secret organization in the communes. That's how you identify yourselves to each other. You drop that line into the conversation somewhere, as though accidently."

Sue Benny said, "What in the name of the living Zoroaster is going on here?"

Ted looked at her. "I'm surprised you're not a member. Bat Hardin is."

"She's not a citizen," Mike said. He moved one hand in a slow graceful motion. "We've got a small autocafeteria in the building. Let's go in and talk. I assume you want to talk."

"Yes, I want to talk," Ted said. "You're obviously some sort of higher-up in this outfit."

Ted and Sue Benny followed the news commentator down a hall to the building's little autocafeteria. It had no more than five tables, four chairs about each of them, and was unoccupied at this late hour. Mike Latimer put a finger to his lips as he seated them.

Ted Swain scowled at him. The gesture was the age-old one calling for silence.

While Ted and Sue Benny sat there and watched him, Mike took what looked like a pen from an inner pocket, and went about the room, pointing it here, there, everywhere, and particularly at anything electronic, such as the TV screen, the TV phone. Finally, he returned it to his pocket and joined them.

"Clean," he said.

"What in the hell spins?" Ted demanded. "What's up?"

"That was an electronic mop."

"Mop?"

"To detect if the room is bugged. It isn't. But these days you can't tell where the National Security Forces will put a bug. They have their work cut out getting them into the communes, but they try, they try. By the way, you've got a bug on you. Do you mind deactivating it?"

Ted Swain put his left hand up under his lapel and flicked off his recorder.

"Coffee?" Mike said.

They both nodded and he dialed coffee for all three, while saying, "If Johnny, the technician, comes in, don't worry. He belongs to the underground too."

Ted Swain looked at him. "What underground?"

"The revolutionary underground." Mike Latimer let air out, then went on. "Obviously, you've come up with the fact, as a result of your prying around in the communes, that there is some sort of underground. Wizard. Let's have some facts, Ted. What kind of government would you say we had?"

Ted Swain grimaced. A lot of curves were being thrown very fast. He said, "Why, actually, it's a sort of dual government. A political one largely based on the

170

old Constitution, though considerably altered at the Second Constitutional Congress, and an economic one headed by the Production Congress, which plans production, communication, transportation, distribution and so forth."

"Yes," Mike said. "And we democratically elect our political representatives, but the computers select, supposedly based on Ability Quotient, those who are to hold positions in the economic field."

"What do you mean, *supposedly*?"

The other came to his feet and paced back and forth in front of Ted, massaging a temple with the tips of his fingers. He was frowning.

"Can't you see?" he demanded. "We continue to think of our society as a democratic one, in which we cherish our freedoms. But the political part of our dual government has become all but meaningless. They continue to play the game, to pay lip service to democracy so that we'll be appeased, but the real clout is held by the economic division. Who controls industry—and when I say industry I, of course, include education, health, entertainment, and all necessary types of work—controls the country. And that in spite of whoever we might vote in as President, Senators, Representatives or whatever."

Ted Swain said impatiently, "But what's this suggestion that the computers don't select workers for industry based on Ability Quotient?"

"Oh, they do, they do, on the lower levels. No reason why not. If you need someone to supervise a line of automated textile-producing machines, or someone to tutor on the grammar-school level at a TV school, or someone to monitor a half dozen laser moles in the Mining Guild, then the computers come up with the very best person available."

"But ... ?"

"But anyone competent to operate a machine can figure out some manner of gimmicking that machine, and the computer is only a machine."

He sat down again, across from Ted Swain.

171

"You mean . . . ?" Ted said.

"Yes. The National Data Bank computers can be and are being gimmicked."

"By whom?"

"By those who would profit, obviously. By those in the highest brackets of our society. By men like Englebrecht, Dollar and Neville, in this region, by their equivalents in other parts of the country. And, by the way, with the full knowledge of the politicians, who themselves are part of the power elite. It's true that in our ultrawelfare society no one goes without. But man doesn't live by bread alone. Our New Class has power, privilege, public esteem, and they wish to keep these and pass them on to relatives and friends. And today they're doing it. And, as with every other class in power in the history of class society, they're willing to do anything to maintain their positions."

"So, this commune underground of yours; what does it want to do?"

"Carry on to the next level in the evolution of society. First, simply eliminate the vestiges of a socioeconomic system based on political division. Remember the royal family and the other feudalistic remnants in Great Britain when you were a boy? They were an anachronism. They were of no value to the nation but they hung on for a century after they had become worthless before the British eliminated them. That is what we plan to do with the remnants of the political state; eliminate it."

"And democracy along with it?"

"No. We plan to transfer democracy to the economic sphere. We think that officials in industry should be democratically elected, from the bottom up, rather than by the computers. Sure, we'll keep some of the aspects of Ability Quotient. A person wouldn't be eligible to run for an administrative position unless he held the qualifications. But the final decision as to who holds a post would be in the hands of his colleagues, not some machine that could be gimmicked."

"So where do things stand now?"

Mike shrugged. "The communes are beginning to oppose the regimentation imposed on them by present society, the political state and the computerized National Data Banks. They want to go to hell in their own way."

"It sounds to me like you're anarchists," Ted muttered.

"Yes, I suppose so, if you want to call it that. We prefer the term 'libertarians.' Say 'anarchist' to most people and they think in terms of bomb-throwing fanatics."

Ted Swain thought about it. He said finally, "So Englebrecht, among others of this New Class, attempt to infiltrate the communes, to track down this movement, by sending in such persons as myself to spy. I might have suspected sooner that it had to be you tipping them off to me in places such as Jissom and New Woodstock. You were the only one I told about it."

"That's right. Every commune in this vicinity now knows about your connections with Neville and Dollar."

Ted Swain said bitterly, "And Gerald Fry. I assume his death was no accident. You people set up the accident."

"Gerald Fry?" Mike shook his head in puzzlement. "We just today got word from Denver members of the underground that he was on his way to this area. I didn't even know he was dead. But you're wrong. Our people wouldn't do a thing like that. Not even those hotheads in Jissom."

Sue Benny spoke up. "Just when do you expect to pull off this revolution of yours? It sounds like a bad scene to me. Not being an American, I'd just as well shirk off and be somewhere else."

He looked at her ruefully. "This type of change is almost always a bad scene. Though in our case the people, as a whole, outnumber the so-called New Class by more than ten to one. We'll prevail. When? I don't know. We're in our infancy so far as organization is concerned. That's why they're so anxious to get in-

173

formation about us. They want to grind us out before we get going. Meanwhile, we need some sort of a spark. Some overt act on their part, perhaps, to coalesce our somewhat differing groups. Something like the Boston Massacre was to the first American Revolution."

Ted Swain stood wearily. He said, "I guess that's about it. Let's go, Sue Benny."

Mike Latimer looked after them as they left, his face thoughtful. Had he said too much? He didn't know where Ted stood.

When they got back to the car, Ted Swain used the TV phone before dialing West Hurley. He put a call through to the apartment of Academician Englebrecht. He didn't expect the other to be available at this hour of the night, so he left a message requesting an interview at ten the following day and urged that, if possible, George Dollar and Henry Neville be present as well.

"What do you plan to do?" Sue Benny said.

Ted saw a faint, rapid pulse fluttering in her temples, struggling for release like a bird in a net. She was obviously anxious for him. Her hands were locked tightly together in her lap.

"I don't know," he said simply as he dialed West Hurley as the car's destination.

In the morning he called the Englebrecht apartment again and got Brian Fitz. Yes, the academician was expecting him at ten o'clock and, yes, he was going to attempt to arrange for Neville and Dollar to be present. The secretary had worked his lips in and out coquettishly and called him 'Ted.' The hell with it.

He decided that there was no point in taking Sue Benny with him. The more she kept out of the public eye in this vicinity the better. It was one thing taking her up to Walden, but the mobile art colony was parked only a few miles from West Hurley and there was a possibility that Neville's men were on the lookout for her. He warned her to hide in the bedroom if a stranger's face appeared on the door's identity screen.

174

She kissed him good-bye before he left, then stepped back and put her hands on his shoulders. He could see anxiety deepening in the frown that shadowed her eyes, but she said lightly, "Take care. And if they give you any sort of a razzle tell them to get goosed."

He laughed sourly. "I'll do that."

On the way over to the university city and its hi-rise administration building, he felt a cold flutter in his stomach. There were all sorts of ramifications to this and he didn't like any of them.

His progression to the escape room of Academician Englebrecht was a duplication of that of his first interview, when his director of dissertation had come up with what, at the time, Ted had thought a brainstorm. Had it been less than a week ago? It seemed impossible. His life had been changed so radically in the past few days. And he suspected strongly that it was going to be changed even more before this day was out.

Brian simpered as he led Ted Swain down the hall to his superior.

He said, "The academician is quite puzzled ... Teddy ... about your desire to have Director Neville and Academician Dollar present." He hesitated. "I do hope we can have a chat before you leave. We have so much in common."

"Yeah, wizard," Ted muttered.

All three were seated when he entered. The ferretlike Neville, the lardy George Dollar, the pompous, beaming Englebrecht. And the eyes of all three were narrowed at him.

Neville was the first to speak. Yes, he was surely of the ferret family, with his pale, pointed face and quick, probing eyes. He spoke, as always, in oblique and nervous bursts, attacking the silence as if it were an enemy, his twisting scornful lips partially obscured by his graying mustache.

He said, "You've found out something important?"

Englebrecht puffed out his cheeks and said, "Of course, of course, he has. Sit down, my boy."

Ted sat and his eyes went about them. "Yes, I have."

175

He looked at Neville. "When you first told me that you thought the communes were hotbeds of subversion, I thought you were slightly drivel-happy and I continued to think so through the first half dozen I investigated. But you were right. Not that I'm revealing anything. You knew you were right. I'm far from the only supposed innocent that you had spying on the communes."

They watched him silently.

He said, "I have no proof but I suspect you people are running scared enough to engineer such matters as the accident to Gerald Fry. He must have found out the true nature of his supposed assignment to investigate the drug culture, and revolted. Possibly he intended to go over to the communes and spill what information he had about you people. Possibly he discovered more than I know. Be that as it may, I realize now that it was also someone from your National Security Forces who twice burglarized my house. It's the only possible way that the identity screens wouldn't report picking up a visitor in my absence. You simply erased such a report. I imagine it was a matter of you not trusting me to submit to you everything I found out, and you sent a man in to check my notes and anything else he could find pertaining to my prying."

Englebrecht snorted. "What are you talking about, Swain?"

"I'm talking about the fact that there is an underground and they're opposed to your manipulating the National Data Banks computers to keep yourselves in power."

Dollar said heavily, "Oh, you are, eh?"

Ted looked at him. "Yes, obviously. And, obviously, I object as strongly as they do. I object to the fact that a Franz Englebrecht can continue to head the Ethnology Department of University City V11, while I'm kept from taking my academician's degree."

They looked at him for a long silent period.

Englebrecht said finally, benignly, "See here, my boy. We must be realistic, of course. There are some people meant to rule, born to rule, and some meant to be ruled. It has always been so. What you must realize is that you are now in a position to join the ranks of those who rule."

"By doing what?" Ted said. "My cover has been blown in every commune within hundreds of miles. They were aware of what I was really doing—stooging for you hombres—before I realized it myself."

Neville said, "There are other regions where you're unknown. We can give you a new identity. You're a natural for this sort of work. You are the most unlikely-looking agent ever. You radiate honesty, good will; you inspire confidence. We need continued information on these radicals. We've got to keep track of what they're up to, nip their movement in the bud."

George Dollar spoke up, his voice unctuous. "See here, Doctor Swain. We all know how ambitious you are, how hard working and competent. Very well, we will let you in on a secret. Shortly, a new amendment to the Constitution will be offered to the Civil Congress. In the future, no one will have the franchise save those who are usefully employed, those who have been selected by the National Data Banks computers, on the basis of their Ability Quotients, to serve this, our great nation."

Ted Swain stared at him. "That would disenfranchise nine tenths of the citizens of voting age!"

Englebrecht nodded. "Of course, of course. And rightfully so. The common herd has no ability to make decisions, not even the ability to decide who should govern them. The new amendment will put all government into the hands of the elite."

Ted said flatly, "And then the new government will see to it that it perpetuates itself."

Neville said, "To the victor belongs the spoils and we are the victors, Swain. We have fought our way to the top and we intend to stay there. In all ages, the best men have come to the top and it is up to them to rule."

Ted Swain said emptily, "Or, if they aren't the best, once they get to the top, by whatever means, they can proclaim themselves to be and liquidate anyone who says otherwise."

Neville said sharply, "We have made you an offer, Swain. Come in with us, or you'll be on the shit list."

Englebrecht said, still benignly, "Do not, and I am afraid, of course, that you'll never get your academician's degree, my boy." He beamed encouragingly. "With it, I am sure certain, ah, arrangements could be made for you to take over the department upon my retirement."

"I'm afraid that under these circumstances I don't want the degree," Ted said emptily.

Neville said, his voice full of wasps, "It goes further than that, Swain. In the building that houses my offices for this region we have one elevator that is not automated—for certain security reasons. How would you like it if at the next muster day you were selected for the job of running it?"

Ted looked at him. This was too much. He had been played like a great, mindless fish. The thought stirred an impotent anger in him. Played like a fish ... allowed to swim about in pointless circles, sweetly ignorant of the hook planted in his mouth.

He said, "If I'm selected for that job, I won't take it."

Englebrecht said, "My boy, my boy. And lose your citizenship rights? Lose your Universal Guaranteed Income? Come now, of course, of course, you'll come in with us."

"No. Of course, of course, I won't. Certain beliefs I've had, certain ideals, have died here today. But not all of them. Good afternoon, you funkers, and you can all go get spayed."

He came to his feet, swept past a fast-blinking Brian Fitz and pushed through the door.

In an inner rage, he stormed down through the building and summoned an electrosteamer. He put his transceiver in its payment slot and dialed West Hurley. At least he'd still have his credit until next muster day, which wasn't far off. Then, when he turned down the elevator-operator's job, they'd cut him off from income, which meant more than just poverty in this supposed ultrawelfare state, this utopia. It meant beggardom.

AFTERMATH

Ted Swain, flanked by Sue Benny, stood before Bat Hardin, town cop of New Woodstock. The other eyed him scornfully.

"So, you've got the gall to come back here?"

"Yes," Ted Swain said simply.

"Well, shirk off before you get hurt."

Sue Benny said, "Bat, don't be a funker. Why do you think he'd come if he didn't have something worthwhile to tell you?"

Bat Hardin looked at Ted Swain, his dark features empty. "Tell me what?"

Ted said, "I've still got enough pseudodollar credit to take Sue Benny and me to Mexico. We'll wait for you there on the other side of the border. By the time they've cut off my Universal Guaranteed Income, as they will, next muster day, we'll be ready to join with New Woodstock for the trip through Latin America. My contribution will be advising on pre-Columbian art. Meanwhile, I'll be writing a book that I've had in mind for years. It needs doing."

Bat Hardin's heavy lips twisted to reveal his scorn. "Like hell you will," he said. "We don't want a fink like you. Why should we support you?"

Ted Swain held out a recording disk. "The last time I saw Mike Latimer, who evidently is some sort of underground official, he said you people needed a spark, confusing as is overt that this New Class pulls that would coalesce the communes. All right. Here it is. I recently had a session with three of the top New Class advocates in this region in which they gave me inside information on what they planned to do in this country, and openly admitting that they manipulated the computers. Give this to Mike and let him begin spreading it around the country."

ABOUT THE AUTHOR

Born in California fifty years ago of stock going back to Gold Rush times, MACK REYNOLDS has made his living as a free-lance writer since 1950, specializing in science fiction. He has published some thirty books and book-length serials and over five hundred novelettes, short stories and articles. In addition, he has co-edited several books, including *The Science Fiction Carnival* (with Fredric Brown), a collection that has been reprinted many times in several languages. Due to a life-long interest in socioeconomics, he has specialized in his extrapolations into the future on themes based upon political economy. Coming to the conclusion that every science fiction writer should have a specialty and deal with a field in which he is knowledgeable, Mack Reynolds has decided to concentrate on the year 2000 and for some time has attempted to write "realistic" science fiction dealing with the problems that will confront us at that time. So successful has he been that organizations such as EIDOS, the Theoretical Research "think tank" specializing on the world of tomorrow, has asked him to become a member. Realizing that books alone are inadequate for research, Mr. Reynolds in the 1950's began a campaign of seeking out material for his stories all over the world and, since, has lived in or traveled through more than 75 countries in every continent but Antarctica. A true adventurer, he once crossed the Sahara to Timbuktu and on the way was captured by the Tuareg (The Forgotten of Allah, and the so-called Apaches of the Sahara). Another time in the tropical jungles of Mexico he was bitten by a vampire bat and had to be treated for rabies. During his travels, Mack Reynolds has been in more than half a dozen wars, revolutions and military revolts, ranging from being shot at by the Huks in the Philippines to being bombed by anti-Castro Cubans. During the Second World War, after graduating from the Army Marine Officers' Cadet School and then the Transportation Corps Marine Officers'

School, he became a second officer (navigator) on Army transport class ships and served in the South Pacific. Later he was offered a soldier of fortune position by Chiang Kai-shek. He says he has been in more jails than he can count off-hand "but never for a dishonorable reason." Although not at the present time affiliated with any political group, he has written books and stories extrapolating on what the future would look like if the Technocrats, Anarchists, various varieties of Socialists, Fascists and other reactionary groups were to realize their dreams. Besides all of the science fiction magazines (especially *Astounding,* later renamed *Analog Science Fact and Science Fiction,* to which he contributed on a frequent basis), his stories and articles have appeared in publications ranging from *Playboy* to *The New York Times.* Today, *persona non gratis* in Morocco, Algeria, Syria, Libya, Egypt, Jordan and Saudi Arabia, he makes his home in San Miguel de Allende, Mexico.

www.ingramcontent.com/pod-product-compliance
Lightning Source LLC
Chambersburg PA
CBHW020638180626
46816CB00003B/1028